Galaxy Gladiators Alien Abduction
Twelve
By
Alana Khan

C000283516

WarDog

Copyright

Acknowledgements

You know that saying 'it takes a village'? Well it seems like I needed one on this book. I had a lot of great feedback. My thanks go to Dr. Lee who donates her time to read the book many times and gives me innumerable suggestions to improve the writing. She had some great ideas about WarDog and Bayne's internal dialogue. Go you, Lee!

My daughter, an author in her own right, Amarra Skye is full of plot help as always. My lovely assistant from across the pond, Stephanie A. who reads and re-reads and helps with a thousand other details. My friend Kassie K. who helps with plotting and always figures out a way to cram more sex into every book—I'm sure my readers thank you, Kassie.

Do you know I have three teams of early readers? My alpha and beta teams read the books to help find plot holes and bloopers. My many thanks to: Sue P., Karla, Carla, Tammy, Karen, Linda P., Kimber, Betty R., Shardae, Lori L., and Corda. I'm juggling a lot of plates and hope I didn't miss anyone!

Interested in being an early reader? Contact me at alanakhanauthor@gmail.com

Want the latest on all the news about the Alanaverse? Newest cover reveals? First chapters? Pictures of the hero's masculine equipment? Sign up for my newsletter at https://alanakhan.com/free-copy-2/ You'll get a free novelette about Shadow's backstory, too. It's crammed full of sex and violence. What would be wrong with that?

Table of Contents

Present Day
Somewhere in Space

There is a Who's Who at the end of this book

Chapter One

Willa

The air is redolent with humid warmth as I wander through a dense forest crowded with tall, leafy trees. A few faint shards of light drift through the thick canopy and dapple the ground, but it's dim down here on the forest floor.

The smell is rich and fertile with decomposing leaves. Birds call to each other from up above. I feel protected in the gloom. The safe cocoon blankets me and I feel my body stand down for what feels like the first time in months.

A huntsman approaches. Because I'm feeling safe here, surrounded by the peaceful ambiance of the forest, I don't startle, I just watch him. He's tall and powerful, his erect posture shouting his control. Brown hair streaked with auburn reaches halfway down his back. An animal pelt is thrown over his shoulders; leather breeches hug his muscular thighs.

His face holds intelligent golden eyes that are keenly interested in me. His lips are full and sensual. The first thought arrowing into my brain is to wonder what it would be like to kiss those lips. By the way his gaze caresses my face, I think he's wondering the same thing about me.

A small smile tips the corners of his mouth even as he slows his approach, then stops. A sound vibrates from deep in the back of his throat as he waits expectantly. Though not a word has been exchanged, I know he's waiting for me to bridge the distance between us.

Feeling no fear, I edge closer. With each step, his appealing looks become more apparent. Tanned skin, wide shoulders, rippled abdomen with what appears to be warpaint, and trim hips beckon me.

The stirrings of desire build low in my pelvis, then swirl there, gathering strength until I feel the drumbeat of arousal lower, as it pulses in my clit.

A dim recess of my mind wonders why I feel so calm, why I have no fear, but I continue to approach him until we're almost toe to toe. I look up into his face and notice the sharp planes of his cheekbones, the warm gold of his eyes.

After laying down his bow, he grips both of my shoulders in his huge, calloused hands. Everything about him is warm, not just the expression on his face, but his skin—heat radiates off him.

My nipples prick, desperate to be held in his large palms.

A little moan escapes me as he wordlessly dips his head toward me, eliminating the distance between us. When he finally kisses me, just a simple kiss, just lip on lip, I moan even louder as I release everything I've been holding back for so long.

Gone is the tightly wound woman who never wanted to share herself with anyone. I banish her, wishing for the briefest moment I could slay her. I want this, and make the conscious decision to allow it.

He pulls my shirt over my head and tugs my pants off before I'm truly aware it's happening. I'm not embarrassed, though. On the contrary, I'm enthralled. He proceeds more slowly as he removes his leather loincloth. As impatient as he was to see me, it's as if he's allowing me time to savor his body.

And savor I do. With every mouthwatering inch he reveals, my body's need spikes higher.

He cocks an eyebrow in silent question as if to ask if I want this. I soundlessly nod. Part of the magic of what's happening is that we haven't exchanged a word.

Dipping his mouth to the curve of my neck, he kisses, then licks, then bites me there. I feel his sharp canines before I see them. He pulls his head back to gaze at me, then allows his lips to curl into a wider smile than he showed before. He's getting all the preliminaries out of the way, attempting to ease all my fears by exposing long, vicious white teeth.

Does he think they might frighten me? They don't. I find them attractive. They're different, tempting. I want to know how they'll feel on my tongue, or lower, when that soft-lipped mouth explores me in other ways.

To answer his silent question, I approach him. Leaning on tiptoe, I slide my arms around his neck and pull him closer for another kiss. Within a moment, our tongues mingle and I learn how to avoid his deadly canines in order to garner pleasure, only pleasure.

His fingers tighten around my shoulders as he pulls me as close as two people can be. His head moves, dipping and bending as he plies me with kisses.

My mind is in too many places at once. I'm loving his mouth on mine and the war he's waging as we thrust and parry. I'm also noticing the tight points of my nipples as they drag against the warm skin of his chest.

When his leg bends and he nestles his thigh between my legs, nudging them apart, then pressing on my clit, I think I'll lose my mind. I don't though, I just moan, then dip my legs to gather more pressure from his obliging leg.

He slides his hands from my shoulders, down my back, and along my sides to my breasts. His thumbs strum my hardened buds in unison, causing me to suck in a surprised breath as pleasure bursts throughout my body.

Now he's plucking them, and the feeling is so intense they ache from the exquisite pleasure.

We could go on like this forever—it feels that good—but I don't want to. I want release. Urgently.

My hands have been lodged on his chest, but I liberate them from their perch and allow their slow slide down soft skin covering solid muscle. They travel southward, over hardened male nipples and rippling washboard abs, following the happy trail of hair below his navel until they find the prize. The proud staff jutting between us.

I smile in realization when I find it's too thick for my fingers to reach around. While avoiding speech, I relay my appreciation with a feline noise of pleasure. He rewards me with a hard kiss on my lips and another nip of those sharp teeth on the column of my throat.

My hand still on his granite-hard cock, he grips my thigh, then glides higher. His hand slips between my legs, and one finger slides between my damp folds. He grunts his pleasure as his fingers slick along the slit, lubricating the way.

One finger enters me, then another, as he develops a rhythm. My hand abandons its post on his cock and my nails bite into his pecs, then I tip my head back, letting it loll there as I bask in his ministrations.

I try not to marvel at his dexterity as he presses into me with two fingers while his talented thumb swipes in circles at the side of my clit.

My gaze finds his as I pant in pleasure. Lifting one leg and pressing my heel against the back of his thigh, I open myself to his attentions until the passion swirling inside me increases and doubles and redoubles until I can't hold back the tides any longer.

I'm bowled over by the force of my orgasm as it sweeps through me like a tidal wave. It doesn't build in increments. No, it slams into me, crashes over me, and pulls words from my mouth even though I hadn't wanted to speak.

"Oh! Good! Oh!" The words mean nothing. They're mindless expressions of my pleasure.

Just as my muscles relax, shoulders sagging, my leg traveling back to the ground, he grunts, nips his canines along my shoulder, and his fingers start their assault again.

I circle my arms around his neck, his body dipped low enough for me to easily reach, and give myself over to the magic of his hand.

With his thumb circling and his fingers pounding into me, my next orgasm barrels at me so fast I don't even know it's coming until it bursts through me like a supernova. My muscles grip deep in my pelvis, then the spasms radiate throughout my body. My teeth clench and my toes curl with the force of the pleasure slicing through every cell of my body.

Before the bliss completely dissipates, I grip his cock and nudge it right where it belongs.

"Yes," I say.

He eases himself into my warm, wet, waiting channel as I feel every inch of him. He's hot. And big. So big I have to widen my stance and tip my pelvis forward to make his entry easier.

The feel of him inside me is paradise. That first breach as he stretches me is almost enough to put me over the edge again. My focus is singular as my mind follows his progress, noting every bump and ridge as well as the burn of acceptance as I open myself to him.

He stands taller and lifts me as if I'm light as a leaf on the wind. I grip his shoulders and hang on for the ride as he pounds into me. Our gazes lock for a moment, then he tips his head back in ecstasy, still thrusting in a rhythm as old as time.

My sensitized clit feels every slide and grind as he impales himself on me over and over. With every plunge, I feel his hot length and girth. All I need to do is decide I want to come, and I fly over the edge again. As soon as I find the energy to open my eyes, I see the grimace of pleasure squeeze his face as he releases into me with a growl.

Dipping his head, he bites my shoulder with lip-covered teeth. Perhaps it's because I don't protest, but he peels his lips away and allows his sharp canines to score me. Two razor-thin lines mark my pale flesh. He tries to hide the smallest smile, proud of the symbol of his possession. I like it, too.

I'm boneless. I lay my head on his chest and allow myself a moment to bask in this pleasure.

Maybe it's a noise that awakens me, or maybe my mind refused to allow me one more moment of the peace and joy this dream provided.

My eyes fly open, regretfully informing me I'm back in my cabin on board the *Fool's Errand*. Immediately, my thoughts slip into normal Willa mode. I want to scold myself for my sexy dream, figure out what time it is, and hurry to the shower to get ready for another day aboard this vessel.

Maybe it's that the dream was too exquisite, too perfect, but I refuse to jump into my workday routine. I decide to give myself a few minutes of pleasure, as if the huntsmen himself gave me permission.

My hand sneaks between my legs, finding myself drenched and ready. My little clit is plump and aroused. Grazing my fingers across it, I find it's shockingly sensitized. I circle my clit, just as the huntsman did in my dream. Closing my eyes I order my body to relax and enjoy this. Being able to give myself pleasure isn't a crime, I remind myself.

Although my mind just had several mind-bending orgasms, my body is still desperate for release. It's the work of a moment to circle my clit, pressing just a bit harder in increments until I allow myself the gratification of flying over the edge.

This time, the release isn't imaginary. My muscles spasm in bliss as they clench and release in a banquet of pleasure.

I float back into my body, open my shuttered eyes, and see WarDog, paws on the bed, huge face an inch from mine, head cocked in interest. His hot breath fans my face.

"WarDog! Once every week or so you've got to give me ten minutes of alone time. Ten minutes! It's all I ask."

He inches closer and nudges me with his soft, wet black nose. Somehow, that doesn't seem like enough of an apology.

Now that I'm fully awake, all the circumstances of my life come crashing back to me. Three months ago I was stolen from my bed in Benson, Texas, and crammed aboard an alien transport ship.

Aliens, yeah. Who knew? Well, actually, I'd always believed in them, but the reality that they existed was still a shock. The tusky boar-like aliens, called Urluts, stole me and transferred me to a different vessel for transport to auction.

It was on that ship where I met a few gladiators, another Earth girl, Aerie, and WarDog. The five of us were rescued by the good people of this ship.

People. It's a term I guess I should use loosely. There are a bunch of Earth women on board. All of us were abducted at various times. All the males, though, are aliens. The males hail from every nook and cranny of the galaxy, most are different species from each other. They have one thing in common; they were all gladiator slaves.

Most of the people on this ship were imprisoned on a slave ship less than a year ago and somehow overthrew their masters. Many of them have become couples over the months they've been together.

Rather than focus on the fact that I could be back in my real life in Texas, I try to thank my lucky stars every single day that I was rescued from slavery and am aboard this ship as a free woman.

We travel the galaxy trying to earn enough credits to evade our former owners, the MarZan cartel, who are still looking for us.

Many of the males still fight in gladiatorial matches to earn money, though no one fights to the death. There are other matches, where the stakes aren't that high, where they get to display their prowess and earn credits. Some don't want to fight anymore, so they've found other ways to contribute, but the ones who do compete seem to enjoy their gladiatorial bouts.

A few of the women earn money, like Grace who sells her music. Aerie has made herself indispensable by wangling more credits for the gladiators' matches. She uses the negotiating skills she honed as an attorney back on Earth.

And me? I'm still flailing. I help out everywhere I can—the laundry, the kitchen, cleaning. Everyone reassures me that my contribution is enough, but I never quite believe that.

I'm most at home helping Star in the hydroponics labs on both ships. I loved working in the garden and fields back in Texas, and although I love nurturing plants and helping them grow, hydroponics doesn't feel right. There's just something about digging in the dirt that soothes my soul.

It's not just *my* ability to stay on this ship that's on the line, I feel responsible for WarDog.

The Urluts threw us all into the same cell together. I had just woken up on board a slave ship guarded by hideous boar-like creatures who slapped a pain/kill collar around my neck and forced me into a cell in the belly of their space vessel.

My heart was jackrabbiting fast enough to make me wonder if I was having a heart attack before I looked up to see who I had to share my cell with. There was Beast, a wall of green flesh standing in one corner, assessing me with intelligent eyes. I later learned he was a gladiator through the translator mechanism I'd been implanted with.

On one of the two bunks was Ar'Tok, a pale alien also described as a gladiator. His eyes flicked to me and then he busied himself studying the floor.

More terrifying and intimidating than either of the huge, muscled gladiators, though, was the furred beast who didn't have the good manners to hide in the corner. It was a dog bigger than anything I'd ever seen on Earth, at least half again as large as a Saint Bernard. His body was brindle, chocolate, and auburn. There was something almost leonine about him because of the way his wild auburn mane haloed his face.

I'm not certain what scared me more, his size, his two-inch-long fangs, or the four-inch spikes on his metal collar.

My hands trembled and my eyes bulged as the animal approached me. Standing, his head almost came up to my shoulder.

He seemed intent on coming closer, and I backed as far from him as I could, my back slamming into the barred metal door. With nowhere to go, I stood paralyzed as he shambled toward me.

"No!" I said with my palm raised toward him. My mouth was so dry the word came out as no more than a breath.

He immediately dropped to the floor, then crawled on his belly the rest of the way so as not to frighten me. He nudged his soft, wet nose under my open palm, wanting me to pet him. His luminous golden eyes spoke wordlessly to me, and the second time he prodded me, I obliged. We've been inseparable ever since.

I didn't know what to call him, and he was in a cell with two gladiators. The ferocious teeth and spiked collar made me wonder if he was bred to fight in the arena like my two humanoid companions. I called him WarDog and the name stuck.

I've always had a love of animals. It started before I was old enough to join the FFA, Future Farmers of America. After I became a member, they taught me animal husbandry and agriculture.

I loved all of it, the gardening, canning, and animal management, but at some point I decided I wanted to be a vet. The problem was I believed I wasn't smart enough. I'd never been great at school and figured I was destined to have a menial job. It wasn't until my senior year in high school that I was diagnosed with dyslexia.

I'm still a slow reader, the diagnosis didn't fix that, but I realized I wasn't stupid. I really *could* do anything I wanted with my life, which is what my mom told me a million times before she died.

Since high school, I worked at a vet's office, and at nights I relearned all the stuff I should have learned in high school. I was just about to apply to college when the Urluts decided I should get an all-expense-paid trip to outer space.

WarDog eases his humongous body up onto my bed an inch at a time, then his giant tongue gives my cheek a dainty kiss. I swear, he thinks he's a lap dog. He also thinks I'm stupid and don't notice he's encroaching on my territory. How do you tell a two-hundred-pound canine he's relegated to the floor? I haven't figured that one out yet.

"All right, big guy. Kisses it is."

Chapter Two

Willa

It's WarDog's favorite morning routine. He delicately slurps me with his huge tongue, and I furrow my fingers through his thick ruff until they reach his warm skin. He loves the gentle scratch of my nails and especially loves my happy voice when I talk to him.

"Yeah, WarDog. He's a good boy. He deserves pets and kisses," I croon to him.

When we've both had our fill, I kiss his nose one more time and roll out of bed. After I shower and dress, we head to the kitchen where I'll help Maddie the cook prepare breakfast for the Mongol hordes.

Alright, they're not exactly Mongols, or a horde, but you'd never know it by their appetites.

Oh shit. I almost skid to a stop when I notice everyone is already in the dining room. Everyone. It takes my brain less than a second to remember why they're all here this early. The match.

We must have docked in the middle of the night last night. I was too preoccupied with my sexy dream—that was a first, I don't think I ever had one that explicit before—to recall we're on Aeon II for Stryker's match.

WarDog and I hurry to the kitchen, but Maddie isn't here. Furred, feline Captain Zar's mate, Anya, and Callista who's in charge of comms, are cooking. My belly squeezes in guilt—they definitely could have used my help this morning.

Maddie is Stryker's . . . I'm not sure what she is. They're not one of the mated couples like Anya and Zar or former-gladiator Shadow and his adorable mate Petra who has more sass inch for inch than anyone I've ever met. Maddie and Stryker share cabins from time to time, and from what I can tell, Stryker would like it to be more permanent.

Even if they're not mates, Maddie clearly has feelings for him, so I'm sure she's a ball of nerves knowing he's going to fight today.

"Sorry. Sorry," I tell Anya and Callista. "I never oversleep. I don't know why—"

"Don't worry about it," Anya says as she flips pancakes on a griddle, "we've got it covered. Why don't you take a day off, too?"

I protest, but when they insist, I grab a few pancakes for me and a stack for WarDog, return to the dining room, and slide in next to Aerie. Since we arrived on the *Fool's Errand* together, I've always kind of stuck with her. Although she and Beast are a mated couple now, she's actually friendlier than she used to be. Their love has somehow mellowed her. It's as if she's finally at home in her own skin.

Beast was voted Captain on our other ship, *The Devil's Playground*, it's the one the gladiators seized after they rescued us. Normally Aerie would be there with him but she's been here for a few days to negotiate a better fee and higher price for Stryker's match as well as to visit me.

Within an hour, WarDog and I are filing down the ramp along with almost everyone on board. As we pay our entry fee for the matches, the guy at the ticket booth shakes his head.

"You shouldn't be here," the crimson-skinned male's voice is deep and gruff, "contestants enter over there." He points to our left with his lips.

"Me?" I point to my chest as if my word needed clarification. He thinks *I'm* a contestant? Seriously?

"The beast," he clarifies.

"He's my *pet*."

"Okay." He shrugs. "Contestants and their handlers get in free, but it makes no difference to me."

Once we've paid, everyone onboard files in and we find seats along what on Earth would be the Mezzanine railing. All of us, that is, except Dax and Stryker. Dax is Stryker's best friend and will be down in the contestants' area with him until his match.

The arena is ancient, as old as the Colosseum in Rome, maybe older. The beige stone seats are in ringed tiers going all the way up to the nosebleed section. The sand in the arena seems to be made of the same stone as the seats and the structure itself.

Everything would be buff-colored if not for the thousands of patrons filing in. They're aliens of every stripe—literally. And their wardrobes are equally colorful.

Smells of spitted meat assault my nose. I see WarDog sniffing it, his black nose squinching with every inhalation. Maybe I'll buy him a treat when the nearest hawker comes by.

The stadium is filled with the noise of eager fans excitedly talking about the upcoming matches, males and females walking up and down the aisles taking bets, and music that sounds like bad porno pouring from ubiquitous speakers.

Maddie is sitting between Anya and Grace, each of whom is holding one of her hands. It's obvious how much she cares for Stryker, she's pale and worried, her teeth tearing at her lower lip.

Stryker is a muscular male with spotted red skin and heavy scars, especially on his face. I've always liked him. Maybe it's because he's the opposite of me. I'm timid and quiet and think before any word slips from my lips. Stryker is loud and brash and says the foulest, funniest shit that flies through his brain. My filter is on overload, and he doesn't have one. He cracks me up. When I'm with him I always feel a bit less uptight.

"Welcome females and males," the male announcer calls from the podium. He's light blue, with puffy tufts of hair at his jowls and two yellow spots on his cheeks. He's colorfully dressed in what can only be called a dress. Either his deep voice belongs to a woman, or his species has taken the kilt idea to the max.

"Our first match of the day will be a rare treat. Most of you have never seen a Skylosian. Since their planet was decimated, they're incredibly rare. If perhaps you've seen one of these beasts before, I doubt any of you have seen a Skylosian match.

"Don't worry, these beasts will not come to any harm today. Due to the Meretrian Agreement, these beings are not allowed to fight to the death. The first animal to roll onto its back, exposing its neck will be declared the loser.

"Their handlers are at the ready to stop the fight at a moment's notice. Negrid," he announces with a flourish as an animal that looks astonishingly like WarDog enters the arena.

WarDog has been lying quietly at my feet since I've been seated. He's usually content to just hang out with me wherever I am. Now, though, he sits up straight and looks directly out at the action. They're clearly the same species.

Shadow is one seat over from me. From what I've been told, he's fought in every sector of the galaxy for over a decade.

"What is that?" I ask him as I lean over Petra.

"I've never seen that species fight before. He's called a Skylosian."

I pointedly look down at WarDog and Shadow gets the message.

"I guess your friend there is a Skylosian," he confirms with a shrug.

Digging my fingers through the hair on WarDog's ruff, I make sure I go all the way to his skin so he can feel my presence. His muscles are different than a moment ago, tighter. I think I'm anthropomorphizing, imbuing him with human qualities where none exist, but I wonder if he's anxious about what will happen to the canines in the arena.

"Montem," the announcer says as Negrid's opponent enters the ring at a trot, the long, chocolate hair of his mane rustling in the breeze.

The two dogs are kept on long leashes by their handlers, but once they've jogged around the periphery of the arena to excited applause, they're pulled up short and are now facing each other in the middle of the arena.

"At the ready," says the announcer. "Begin!"

The handlers release their animals and step away. They prominently display the equipment, about the size of a cell phone, aloft in their hands. It suddenly dawns on me that whatever the Meretrian Agreement is, it was meant to reassure patrons that the fighting animals won't be harmed.

The paradox is not lost on me that many of the matches here today will pit sentient humanoids against each other and they will fight to the death, but people's sensibilities are offended by the possibility that canines might be harmed. The equipment they're holding up so everyone can see must be a visual signal that they can stop the fight at a moment's notice.

The dogs begin circling each other, growling so loudly I can hear it from here. One of the handlers must give a verbal command, because the lighter of the two, Negrid, appears activated and launches at his opponent.

The fight is on, with neither animal holding back. They snarl as they attack each other. Even though their fur is thick, you can see their power in the way they move. Their hindquarters, sleeker than their fronts, show every muscle as they tuck their haunches beneath them to propel forward with more force.

Mighty jaws, with those long canines I'm so familiar with, are flashing white in the sun as the two animals threaten each other. They're wearing metal collars similar to what WarDog had around his neck when I met him in that cell on the Urlut vessel. The spikes that ring their necks are four-inches long.

Every muscle in WarDog's body is poised to run, or in this case jump. We're maybe sixty feet above the sand, but by the way he's pulling on his leash, I wonder if he wants to leap into the fray.

Shadow and Petra change places to my left so Shadow is sitting next to me. He grabs WarDog's collar, just to lend a hand. In other circumstances, I would protest that I needed no assistance, but I'm glad for the help. If WarDog decided to leap over the three-foot rail, I wouldn't be able to contain his powerful muscles.

The fight in the arena goes on for long minutes in the hot sun, but eventually Montem pounces hard on Negrid's withers and grabs the other's muzzle in his deadly teeth. Negrid rolls onto his back and both handlers intervene.

The controllers must shock the dogs, because both of them stand down immediately. Montem rolls to stand on all fours and the onlookers rise to their feet in applause.

"Females and males," says the announcer, "you can certainly do better than that. Let's show these animals our true appreciation for the battle you just observed."

The noise in the arena rises by a few notches.

"I know you can do better," the announcer goads.

The patrons now go wild as the dogs circle the edge of the arena again. It's as if this is the canine equivalent to taking a bow.

The announcer motions to Montem's owner in a sweeping gesture of his outstretched hand. You can hear the male's microphone being switched on.

"Thank you for coming today," the handler says. He's a bulky male with skin that looks like cooled magma, all rolling black flesh that folds over and over on top of itself. "Montem of Skylose." He lifts both fists in the air as if he himself won the match. "To the victor go the spoils!"

He makes a show of pressing a button on the controller and all at once I'm uncertain what my eyes are seeing. The animal begins to change—his form distorts so quickly I have trouble processing what's happening. Within half a minute, though, Montem is no longer a deadly ball of brown fur and two-inch fangs. Montem has shifted into a humanoid.

Fascinated as I am by the show in the arena, I can't control my gaze from flying to WarDog. If I thought he was stiff during the fight, he was loose compared to this. Every muscle in his body appears to be on high alert as he watches the action in the sand.

He's whining now; it's almost continuous. His leash pulls on my fingers. It's not an overpowering yank, my big boy is too well-behaved for that, but I can feel his yearning to go to the arena.

"Shadow? What the fuck is going on?"

"I've never seen this species before. They're humanoids who shift into canines?" It sounds like he wanted that to come out as a statement, but it certainly sounded like a question to me.

Is there a humanoid trapped in WarDog's body? How could we not have known this? No one on the ship had heard of Skylosians before? If WarDog is this species, then he's humanoid under all that fur. My eyes open wide in wonder as shock spikes through me.

The pomp continues in the ring for a few more minutes, then the combatants along with their handlers exit through the doorway leading to the catacombs.

"Shadow, we've got to get down there. If there's a humanoid under all this fur, I need to talk to those handlers and see how to break the spell."

"I understand. Steele, Aries, come with us."

My three bodyguards and I, along with WarDog, make our way to the nearest steps, then skirt along the rounded walkway to the arched doorway leading to the underground area where the fighters are housed.

As we approach, the two armed guards at the entryway stand taller and try to block us.

"We have business," Shadow says, his tone is firm as he glances at the dog.

"Kin?" one of the guards says with a leer as if it's funny as hell that WarDog might be related to one of the fighters.

"Perhaps. Let us pass." Shadow puffs his chest, his nonverbal suggestion that if the guard doesn't let us through there might be a gladiatorial fight right here, right now. I don't think the guards would like the outcome.

"And her?" one of them says, his eyes sliding to me.

"His handler. Want her to unleash him on you?"

WarDog growls as if on cue, showing more snarling white teeth than he's ever shown me.

We step into the underground area passing from the heat of the sun to the cool of these ancient catacombs. The fetid smell assaults me. The walls are the same beige squares as the rest of the structure. It's cooler down here, but I can't wait to escape the claustrophobia and return to the bright light of day.

About twenty males, all wearing loincloths, line the hallway. Some sit, some squat, some are perched on the few stone benches that must be centuries old. These males must be the rest of the day's entertainment.

I see Stryker on the stone floor, Dax standing next to him as if he's the male's owner. They don't approach us or act as if they know us. It would call more attention to us, which we certainly don't need right now.

Shadow leads us down a hallway, and it suddenly strikes me that all the males with me have probably been in this facility during their careers. They've sat where Stryker's sitting right this minute, possibly about to enter a deathmatch, wondering if they would be alive or dead by sundown.

I'm so glad we've all found our freedom.

WarDog is in the lead now. His more acute sense of smell is pulling him toward the other Skylosians. We pass several rooms, actually more like cubbies, where perhaps the premier acts are allowed to wait before their bouts. Negrid, still in canine form, is in one, not only being verbally eviscerated by his master, but receiving some abusive kicks as well.

I clamp my teeth together, hard, when Shadow spears me with a quelling look. "Don't say anything," he whispers. "Your words will change nothing, and it will call too much attention."

Earth was no picnic, but I have to admit the galaxy is a harsh place.

We find Montem in the next cubby. He's a tall, muscular humanoid with canine aspects to his face—sharp cheekbones, high pointed ears, a swath of fur across his shoulders, and rounded brown eyes. His hands are pressed to the small of his back as he leans backward, moaning in pleasure. I wonder how long he was in his canine form. It must feel odd to walk on two legs again.

Both his and his handler's attention is riveted on WarDog.

"What?" the handler asks roughly. "Want to sell your fighting stock? Highly unusual to approach a handler, especially at a match. Lucky for you I just won and I'm in a good mood."

He didn't just win anything. But I don't say that. Nor do I mention that if this is his good mood I don't want to catch him on a bad day.

I don't let Shadow or any of the males speak for me. Ignoring the owner and stepping toward Montem, I ask, "He's one of you, right?"

He nods, his eyes darting toward his handler. He may be in humanoid form, but he's not a free male.

"Don't be an idiot," the handler scolds. "Of course he is."

"He came to me this way. How do I get him into his humanoid form?"

The handler's eyes narrow to slits. "If you don't know the answer to such a basic question, you can't be his owner," he says.

"He's *mine*!"

"Got his papers?"

"He's a free agent."

"So, what is he? He's yours? Or he's free? You can't have it both ways," the handler jeers.

Shit.

"I think I'll take him off your hands," he says as his jaw clenches.

"You and who else?" Shadow steps up and practically bumps him with his muscular chest. Steele and Aries step closer also. I have no doubt the three gladiators could overpower the handler in a heartbeat.

WarDog chooses this moment to step closer and put a soft mouth around the male's thigh. Out of anyone on the planet, my guess is that this male knows what could happen if WarDog peels back his lips and grips his thigh with those long, white teeth.

"Tell me, male. How do we change the canine into his upright form?" Shadow's tone is harsh.

"Try my controller. Most of the Skylosians were owned by the cartel at one time. They were all chipped with the same hardware."

Shadow grabs the controller and asks, "Which button shocks and which allows the change?"

"Top button shifts, bottom shocks," the male says, spearing him with an angry look.

Shadow presses the bottom button, obviously not trusting the handler to tell the truth. His hunch was right because WarDog shifts before my eyes. The handler roughly snatches the controller back.

WarDog doesn't stand like Montem did, but lies on his side on the stone floor. It's shocking to have a front-row seat to this metamorphosis. The fur covering most of his body disappears, replaced by tanned skin. Brindle fur, the color of WarDog, remains across his shoulders to the top of his pecs on his chest and tapers to a 'V' in the middle of his back.

He curls into a tight ball and groans for a moment. I'm used to every sound WarDog can make, but the male on the floor sounds different somehow, more . . . humanoid.

He's in pain. Montem didn't shift like this. He leapt to his feet before his change was complete. WarDog's metamorphosis is slower and definitely more painful.

He rolls onto his back and slowly unfolds, allowing his spine and hips to fully straighten for the first time since I met him, and who knows how long before that?

His eyes are closed, facial muscles tight, but I can see his humanoid features and totally naked humanoid body for the first time. Perfect rose-colored lips that can't hide the tips of his sharp canines. High, angular cheekbones that hint at what he looks like in his non-human form. And pointed ears much higher on his head than mine. I command myself not to look lower than his chest and have to struggle to obey.

He makes a sound. It's an unintelligible growl. Is he more beast than man? Can he speak? Is he even fully sentient in this form? Montem is capable of thought and speech, but perhaps WarDog isn't.

He growls again, then says, "Willa," as clear as if he'd spoken English his entire life. "Willa," he repeats, his golden eyes never leaving mine. I guess his speech was just a bit rusty.

"WarDog are you okay?" Stupid question, I know, but what do you say at a moment like this?

"Bayne," he croaks in a manner that hints at just how long it's been since he's used his mouth for speech.

"Pain? You're in pain."

He nods, his head barely moving, then points to his chest and repeats, "Bayne."

That's his name. Of course, he has a name other than WarDog.

"How do we get a controller?" I ask the handler, not wanting anything other than to get the fuck out of here before someone detains us or discovers Bayne has no owner and appropriates him.

"The controller is for an owner," Montem offers. By the way his handler's gaze pierces him with lighting bolts, he's risking his safety by telling us this. But he continues, "If he's free, all you need to do is . . ." he moves swiftly and bends to touch the back of Bayne's neck "remove—." He can't finish his sentence. His handler has pushed the button and both Skylosians shift back to their canine forms.

"Bolt!" Shadow shouts as soon as Bayne has fully changed back to WarDog.

Poor WarDog is moving slowly as we try to hustle him out of the underground area. His spine and hip joints must be screaming in pain having been stretched in different directions in such a short span of time.

Shadow reaches down, lifts the huge animal into his arms as if he was carrying a baby, and the four of us race into the sunlight. The rest of our contingent see us fleeing through the arched entryway, and most run to meet us as we leave the grounds.

A few stay to protect Stryker, who still has to compete in his match.

We're running to the *Fool's Errand*, which is parked maybe four city blocks away. At some point, Shadow hands WarDog off to Steele and we all keep hurrying.

Someone must have comm'd ahead, because Dr. Drayke has a stretcher at the top of the ramp as we board.

"I wish I would have known," Dr. Drayke says an hour later after he's removed a small metal device the size of a grain of rice that had been lodged near the top of Bayne's spine. "I would have removed it the same time we removed the spiked collar the day he boarded. I think he'll be fine. Let me go to my lab to examine the controller more closely. I'll leave you two alone."

Bayne is on a bed in his humanoid form. I've been in the room for the entire procedure and when the controller was removed from his spine, I had the opportunity to watch him shift from canine to humanoid again. Now I have the time to inventory him more closely.

He has brown hair with auburn streaks, the same brindle he had in canine form. His ears are closer to the top of his head than at the sides like a human. They're triangular, like a German Shepherd.

He has the same ruff on his shoulders he had in canine form. It's the most obvious characteristic of his dual nature.

Otherwise, his lips are fully human although the long canines peeking out between his lips belie his true origins.

The nails on his hands and feet are humanoid, not resembling claws in the least.

His lids pop open and our gazes immediately lock. His eyes are beautiful. Mesmerizing. They're golden. A warm, almost blazing gold that's so rich and so deep you could dive into them. They are just like WarDog's—this both shocks and reassures me at the same time.

"Willa," he says, the look on his face shows rapidly changing emotions I can't identify. "How long?"

"How long since what?"

"Have I been . . ."

"I've known you three months . . . *lunars*. Before that, I have no idea."

He closes his eyes and blows a long stream of air through his lips.

"I think it was a long time. Long time. I was in my shifted form maybe . . . *annums*. My thoughts are cloudy." He glances around the room as if he's only just noticing it. "Medical?"

"Medbay, yes."

"Did we used to . . . share a room?"

"Yes."

"Can we go back there?"

"Sure," I say before I give much thought to the fact that we shared it when he was WarDog. Now he's Bayne. Very handsome, very masculine Bayne.

For a moment, the way he looks at me isn't humanoid. He's more like a wolf. The wolf in Little Red Riding Hood who wanted to eat her up.

He's looking me up and down with undisguised interest. The blanket covering him tents at his hips.

His nose wrinkles as he pointedly looks at the sterile cabinets. "Can we leave this room?"

"Sure."

I don't know why I'm saying 'sure' when I'm not at all sure this is a good idea. I stand near the bed and let him rest his hand on my shoulder as he rises. He grunts deep in the back of his throat as his feet hit the floor.

"You're in pain?"

"My spine, hips, and shoulders are screaming. I was in my shifted form too long."

Dr. Drayke hears him and comes out from his office with a hypo-gun in his hand. "Can I give you something for your pain?" he asks as he motions with the gun.

When Bayne nods, the doc puts it against his shoulder and there is a hiss as he depresses the trigger. "This will help with the pain and stiffness. Take a hot shower. You'll feel better in about half an *hoara*. Rest today then slowly increase your activity." Bayne nods his thanks and Dr. Drayke returns to his office.

Bayne's naked hip grazes mine with every step as we slowly walk the hallways to my cabin. When I slide my arm around his waist to steady him, I realize how tall he is.

My arm, rather than circling his waist, is beneath it. His skin is hot, warmer than a human's. I'm trying not to stare, but I catch glimpses of him from my peripheral vision. He's tall and tan and perfectly built. His shoulders are wide, his waist narrow, and his hip bones are visible beneath his skin.

It's not his hip bones, though, that fascinate me. It's his cock that has captured my attention. It's bobbing at his hips, semi-hard and huge, jutting from an inviting thatch of brown hair.

Forcing my attention away, I try to find something in the hallway that's half as interesting. Fat chance. I look up to notice we're at our destination.

"Here we are." I palm the entry plate and help him onto the bed.

"Piss," he says, pointedly looking at the bathroom door.

I help him there and leave him at the doorway.

"Gods." I hear a few minutes later. "It's been *annums*, perhaps a decade."

He must have gotten a good look at himself in the mirror.

"I don't know how, can you turn the shower on?" he calls.

My mind is still reeling from this new turn of events. At first, I was consumed with escaping the arena and evading the authorities in case they came to confiscate the male. Then I was fearful as I watched the medbot remove the hardware lodged near his delicate spinal nerves. I never allowed the impact of what happened to actually hit me.

I slip into the bathroom and turn on the shower, then return to plop on the bed. My mind spins until he returns to the room. During the entire time I should have been deciding what to do about the humanoid who's expecting to share my bed, all I could think about was what he might be doing to his cock in the shower, or what I might do to that cock when he returns.

The huntsman! The huntsman from this morning bore a shocking resemblance to Bayne.

How could I have dreamed of Bayne this morning? My mind searches for answers, but I haven't a clue. What I do know is that this Earth girl is on a spaceship a million miles from home. And I know there are dozens, perhaps hundreds of alien species out there whose appearance and powers are things I couldn't have dreamed of.

What I do know is that all the knowledge I possess doesn't fill a thimble. What I do know is that as sure as I'm sitting here, I dreamed about Bayne this morning. And I wanted him. And I orgasmed thinking about him.

The bathroom door opens and Bayne's wide shoulders practically fill the doorway. He's nude. He hasn't even slung a towel around his hips. I guess I shouldn't make too much of that, he hasn't worn clothes for a decade by his reckoning.

"Want a nap? You've been through a lot," I say as I leap off the bed toward the far wall, keeping the bed between Bayne and me.

"Bed. Yes."

He slides between the sheets and gazes at me in silent invitation. There's something about the way he swivels his head that's vaguely canine. I imagine I'll notice a lot of things like that as I get to know him.

"I don't remember much," he says as he pats the mattress, beckoning me. "But I remember some things. I know you petted me all the time. Your touch was soft and gentle. Things in shifted form get fuzzy when I return as Bayne. But I . . . remember this morning."

This morning. This morning's little masturbation session. He watched. As I recall, when I was done pleasuring myself his nose was inches from mine. Great. He remembers that.

Chapter Three

Bayne

I ache. Deep in my bones. The ache is warm and tight and unrelenting. Nothing feels right. My teeth don't seem to fit in my mouth correctly, my fingers feel too long, and all the vivid colors hurt my eyes.

My thoughts are swirling. I vaguely remember people I think were my parents, but my childhood is like a swirling black hole with more questions than answers.

There were so many years in my canine form. By the male's face who looked at me in the mirror, it's been more than a decade. I remember the spiked collar I wore on my neck and the smell of metal that was never far from my nose.

There were fights. I remember those. Perhaps I'm remembering all of them, because there were many. So many. If what I remember is only a portion, I fought a lot. So much blood. Thankfully most of it was my opponents'. I can taste the metallic tang in my mouth. I remember some respite, some moments or days in two-legged form, but so much time was spent on all-fours.

You're back! My inner dog says with joy and excitement. *So much pain. Fight. Kill. Pain.* He is practically howling. *Then Willa came. She saved us. She stroked us and hugged us.*

It's been so long since I could talk to my inner beast I am practically vibrating with joy.

Yes. We're finally free.

This bed is blissfully soft, especially compared to sleeping on the cold stone of cells and cages for the duration of my captivity.

And then there's Willa. Willa of soft hands and softer voice. After so many years in my shifted form, I couldn't think properly, couldn't understand many of her words, but I knew her. I knew she wouldn't hurt me. I felt her caring, her concern.

I know the scent of her arousal. It was strong on her this morning. I remember that. There are things that become fuzzier when I'm in canine form and things that grow sharper. The aroma of excitement is sharp. I can smell emotions.

Since I met her, Willa has reeked of longing and sadness. Her love for me, though, has never wavered.

I sniff in and get a big gust of her scent. It's not full of her love now. It's fearful . . . and aroused.

I'm under the covers but can see the flag of my desire stating the obvious. By the look in her flared brown eyes, she sees it too.

I don't want to think about the last decade. That would make me both melancholy and furious. I'd rather pay attention to the attraction arcing between us like a living thing.

"Willa. Join me," my tone is warm, persuasive.

A picture of what she was doing this morning flies into my mind with as much clarity as anything that happened in my shifted form. How lovely she was when she pressed her head back against her pillow, her mouth open in a small 'o'. The swiftness of her hand circling between her legs. The soft, desperate noises she made when she got close, and the long, low satisfied moan when she reached her climax.

My cock is rock hard when I remember that. My canine nose comes alive beneath my skin as I recreate it in my memory—the spicy bite and allure of her scent. When I glance at her again, I'm sure my desire is clear as my gaze burns through her.

Take her, mate her. My canine whines and nudges. I push him back and assure him that's the plan.

"I could ease you," I say, hoping my voice doesn't sound as rough to her as it does to me. "I could give you more than you gave yourself this morning."

By her reaction, this wasn't the right thing to say. Her lids fly wide, as does her mouth. She paces backward until her back hits the wall. Her small hands fly up, palms toward me as if to keep me away although I'm lying on my back. I doubt she even knows she's doing it.

What did I do wrong? I sniff again, four little breaths and one long one. I'm certain I'm right. The scent of her arousal is thick in the air. There must be something I don't understand. My memories are still shrouded in fog with only little snippets of clarity.

I have no doubt, though, that in my pack, we expressed our desires freely with willing partners in both two- and four-legged form until we mated. Then my species never stray from their mates. In my head WarDog whines in confusion and distress and it's all I can do not to make the same sound out loud.

"Willa?"

"What?"

"I desire you."

"Yeah, that's obvious." Her gaze flicks to the tent my cock is making under the covers.

"You desire me," I point out the obvious, my head cocked because I don't comprehend the problem.

"No. I don't."

I breathe in loudly through my nose. "Yes. You do."

Her eyes prick with tears. She looks surprised and ashamed, then shakes her head.

"You're mistaken. And why are we having this discussion? We just met."

"You said you've known me for three *lunars*."

"Well, yeah . . . No, I've known you for two hours. I knew WarDog for three *lunars*."

"I *am* that canine. Weren't you there when I shifted?"

"We've exchanged maybe a hundred words. All of them in the last few hours. That's how long I've known you." She's angry. I don't understand why. Her mind wants one thing but her body desires something else.

"You're angry. What did I do?"

She takes a deep breath as a thousand emotions flit across her face. They shift from surprise to anger to sadness then circle back to anger.

"We just met. We've known each other for two hours and you've propositioned me. That's rude."

"It is? I smell your need. I offered to ease you." I'm baffled. Perhaps my translator is old and needs an update. But that couldn't be it. I can read the expression on her face without benefit of translation. She's furious, and hurt.

WarDog, as he now wants to be called, is anxious and pacing inside my head. He releases one plaintive whine.

"You do *not* smell my need. That's rude. It is not something we talk about in polite society."

"Okay. I won't mention it again." This conversation is making my head ache.

She dips her face into her hands, her shoulders sagging. I smell her tears. I've made her cry. Willa, the kindest person in my life in the last decade, and I've somehow saddened her by offering to ease her.

I climb out of bed and walk to her, then fold her into my arms.

Bending my head to her ear, I whisper, "I didn't mean to make you cry. I wanted to provide pleasure, not pain."

Instead of comforting her, I hear her sobs. Now I've made her weep. I know I've been in my shifted form for a long time, but did things change that much since I've been gone? How could I make such a mess of this?

"I'm sorry." I pet her head like she's petted mine since I've known her.

"You're naked!" she moans as she presses her palms against my chest and half-heartedly pushes me away.

Trying to comply with her wishes, I take a step back, my head cocked to her level so I can discern what she's thinking.

"You're aroused!" she accuses.

"Yes. You're beautiful." Certainly this compliment should calm her.

"Bayne!" Her tone doesn't sound calmer. She's scolding me and getting angrier.

"I've been away a long time, Willa. Explain what I've done wrong. I only want to ease you."

"Sit!" she orders, pointing to the bed. In my mind, WarDog immediately complies and sits, urging me to do likewise.

I back up until the backs of my legs hit the bed, then sit down.

"No. I mean lie down."

I do.

"Under the covers!" she sounds exasperated.

I climb under the covers, my eyes never leaving hers, assuming there will be another order in a moment, like dance, or twirl in a circle, or make sounds like the tree-dwelling animals that used to jump from limb to limb on Skylose.

"What did I do?" I ask again.

Crying now, she blindly reaches for a chair, pulls it toward the doorway, and sits.

"I didn't know you were a human. I mean a humanoid. I thought you were a dog."

"I understand," I tell her, nodding my head, encouraging her to say more, even as I don't understand at all.

"I . . . told you things. Secret things. Things people don't readily divulge to other people."

Oh. She told me things. My canine brain doesn't really understand a great deal of the higher-level things that happen in my shifted form. It's primitive. It understands raw emotion, strong orders, urgent words, and bodily needs. But everything Willa told me seemed urgent. I remember a lot of what she told me.

"And you watched me . . . darn! I can't even say it out loud."

I watched her pleasure herself. Not just this morning, but many times. I loved watching that. I loved everything about it. I loved the smell, yes, my canine loves many smells, but none more than that. But I loved the way her face flushed. I loved her little moans of pleasure. I loved the way her relaxed muscles felt when she snuggled me afterward. By the look on her face, I get the message I should never bring any of these things up with her. Never.

Willa

Look at his face. Dear God, he's so alien . . . and so handsome. And miserable, as if I've confused him so badly he doesn't know what to do. As much as I'd like to make him into the bad guy, he's not. I'm just so freaking embarrassed.

I should explain this to him. It's just, what do you say? I told you about everything in my entire life thinking I was talking to a dog and it turned out you're a man . . . a male.

I cradle my face in my hands again and breathe, trying to think. By the look on his face, I've confused the shit out of him. I want to help him understand what's going on with me. But before I can do that, my mind has to punish me with a rolling movie of everything I divulged to him over the last three months.

Go ahead, I tell myself. Remind me of all the shit I spilled to him under cover of darkness. There were the things I did that were slightly embarrassing, like cheating in grade school, and saying mean things to schoolkids before I developed a good filter. Those were nothing. I'd feel okay about doing a standup comedy routine about them.

It's the stuff from Junior High and beyond where things get dicey. The fumbled first kisses. The stupid things I told girlfriends that resulted in learning to never tell anyone my deepest thoughts because they would be splattered all over the Junior High grapevine or worse, Facebook, within an hour.

The mortifying first fumblings on second and third base with the wrong boys. Losing my virginity and having it mentioned derisively on social media. I socially hibernated for years after that.

I peek through the gap between my hands to glance at the male on the bed in front of me. He's sitting up against the headboard, just waiting for me. His face is sweet, impassive, as if he'll sit like that all day until I figure out what to do.

And here he is, coming out of a long hibernation of his own. You'd think he'd be more interested in regaining his life, or creating a new one. Anything other than spending his first day back on two legs waiting for a crazy Earth female to explain her seesawing emotions.

"I told you embarrassing things, Bayne. And I masturbated in front of you." There. I said it.

He nods. As if this is nothing. As if I'm telling him what I had for dinner last night. But, of course, he knows that too.

"Just looking at you, knowing you know every embarrassing moment of my life, makes me uncomfortable. I need some time."

"Okay."

Perhaps he doesn't know what that expression means. Any Earth male would know that it's code-speak for 'I'm breaking up with you and you should get out of my fucking bed'. Obviously, the Skylosian did not get the memo, because there's still a tent under the covers and he hasn't moved a muscle. In fact, he's still looking at me expectantly, perhaps waiting for me to join him in bed and let him 'ease' me.

"And it's rude to ask a woman to have sex when you've only known her a few hours. You shouldn't ask me again," I instruct.

"After how many *hoaras* is it not considered rude?"

At this, my mouth actually pops open in surprise. Look at his face! It's so sincere. He doesn't even realize how impolite that question was. Actually, if I allow myself to see it, his artless innocence is endearing. But right now I don't want to acknowledge that.

"So, you're going to pull on some clothes and we're going to march to the bridge and have them assign you a room of your own. You aren't going to be sleeping in my room anymore."

He cocks his head in a very familiar way. He did this as WarDog and it never failed to earn him a pat on his head because he was so adorable. He's definitely adorable now, but I need to force that out of my mind.

"No problem. I can shift back to my canine form and sleep with you that way. I won't ask to share pleasure with you again."

I scan his face, looking for the telltale signs that he's teasing me, but he's so freaking sincere it squeezes my heart.

"Nope. Separate cabins. I just realized you have no clothes. Wait right here and I'll borrow some for you. I'll be back."

I scurry out, palm the door closed, and lean against it as I take deep breaths. My life has spiraled out of control in the span of a few hours.

After borrowing clean clothes from one of the males and getting Bayne a cabin assignment from Callista, I return to find him sitting where I left him. It strikes me that he's been a dog for a long time, forced to sit and wait when ordered to do so.

In fact, I used to do that to him. He'd happily sit and wait for me when I told him to. Until this moment, I've felt guilty for kicking him out of my cabin. Now I realize it's a kindness. He needs to figure out who he is, and he'll never be able to do that living in this room with me.

Chapter Four

One month later . . .

Bayne

"Nice job today," Stryker tells me as I gulp a bottle of water.

I've figured out my body temperature runs hotter than most others on this vessel, perhaps that's why I'm sweating more than my sparring partner. I don't care how uncomfortable I am, though, I work out every day, most days twice.

I like sparring with Stryker, he's an excellent fighter, and patient as can be with me. All the males have pitched in to teach me different skills: the trident, the gladius sword, even chainsticks. I like the broadsword best, though. It feels good in my hands. I like the heft of it, and it's reassuring to sheathe it behind my back when I'm done.

I've taken to walking through the halls of the ship with it, enjoying the weight of it on my back and the feeling of being at the ready. I even shifted with it on once, to make sure I could step out of the sheath and be in shape to fight in my canine form if necessary.

Having fought for so long as a canine, I like owning and carrying metal. It reminds me of all the power I have at my disposal as a humanoid. None of the weapons nor the fighting skills feel familiar to me except for the bow and arrow. The males speculate that I must come from a tribe that were hunters, not warriors. I still don't have any memories of that time but I assume they are correct.

"Are you coming to the party tonight?" Stryker asks as he returns his gladius to the weapons room.

"I . . ." All the power I felt over the last *hoara* as I fought with Stryker drains out of me and WarDog whimpers like a pup. I feel like a youngling again.

"I see how you look at Willa. A blind male could see it, Bayne. Come tonight. Ask her to dance. Hold her in your arms. Who knows, maybe you'll get lucky." He winks at me. His big red body and scarred face could scare a stranger when he does this, but I know he wouldn't hurt anyone unless he's in the arena or in the line of duty as security.

Yes, take her, hold her, make her ours. WarDog encourages as he sits up straighter, ears pricked.

"She wants nothing to do with me. I'll be in my cabin studying my people's history and looking at pictures of my planet. Maybe I'll get my memories back."

"I've watched *her*, too. She ignores you when you're watching, but her eyes follow every move you make when you're occupied. Every. Move. I smell her arousal. I'm surprised you can't since you have a canine nose. You don't smell it bloom whenever you're around?"

"She told me that's not what it is."

Stryker's bark of laughter is so loud it could probably be heard at the other end of the ship. "Just because you find her soft and kind and beautiful doesn't mean she can't lie, Bayne. Her lips might tell you she's not interested, but her body is shouting its desire."

"Really?" *Yes, yes, yes,* agrees WarDog.

I figure I'm in my late twenties, but much of the time I feel at least a decade younger. My *annums* in my shifted shape were lost in many ways. I didn't grow up. Stryker's female, Maddie, tells me this last *lunar* has been an 'emotional growth spurt' for me. She's befriended me in many ways including cooking special dishes for me.

Perhaps I should have known Willa was lying when she denied her interest, or maybe Stryker doesn't know what he's talking about.

"Come tonight my friend, or Maddie and I will show up at your door and drag you. Wear the black leather kilt Dax helped you make. The females seem to love when we wear them. See you tonight."

He strides out of the *ludus* where we've been sparring, leaving me alone in here. My thoughts stray to the morning in Willa's cabin before we went to Aeon II. I replay the moments when her hand furiously circled her sex under the covers. The scent of her pleasure was so rich it's as if I can still smell it. Even now, my ears ring with every remembered pant and moan.

I want that again. No. Not that. I don't want to be covered in fur and lurking on the sidelines. I want to be a Skylosian male whose cock brings her pleasure. I want her wrists securely bound in my hand so she has to rely on me and only me to make her come.

The only way to do that is to show up at the dance tonight and let her see I'm not the compliant pup I was when she met me. In my mind, WarDog gives an enthusiastic woof of encouragement.

Willa

I check my image in the mirror once more, even as I shake my head, disapproving of this whole idea. I had no intention of going to the party tonight. Everyone on board is paired up in one way or another. From mated pairs to occasional sex partners. And then there's me. And Bayne.

He's changed a lot over the last month. My mouth quirks in the mirror, amplifying my dismay. He's no longer the male who sat paralyzed in my bed awaiting my return a month ago, willing to follow my every command as if he was still a canine.

No. Now I watch him stride through the hallways with a sense of purpose, sometimes with a wide sword on his back as if he's Conan the Barbarian. He's powerful, and sexy, and . . . no longer interested in me.

I sent him away. If I'm honest with myself, I'll admit I assumed he'd still want me and would be ready when I got over my little snit and asked to spend time with him. Well, the joke's on me.

His eyes don't shine brighter when I'm around, nor do they follow me around the room. He seems more interested in joking with his buddies or talking to the other women than in being with me.

He acts like a sponge, wanting to learn everything, making up for lost time. It still makes me sad that he has so much lost time to make up for.

He's learning a few cooking skills from Maddie who treats him like a brother. Grace has taught him the basics of playing a stringed instrument, although they both decided he'll never have musical talent. Dax's mate Dahlia is teaching him to read because he either doesn't remember, or his people were too primitive to have written language. He's already tearing up the Intergalactic Database learning more about his home planet.

My brief investigation of Skylose revealed it was decimated by war shortly after he was abducted and permanently forced into his canine form. The history of his race is sad and I decided I knew enough after only a few minutes of research. The fact that everyone he ever knew is probably dead and gone might explain the somber look I see on his face from time to time.

I barged into the *ludus* a few days ago, searching for Dax because I wanted him to teach me how to make a new pair of shoes. He's handy with everything he touches, including wood and leatherwork.

I thought I could just make an appointment for us to meet later and then leave. Of course, he just happened to be sparring with Bayne. I stood near the doorway and watched until Dax stopped to ask me what I needed.

I can replay every second of their match. By heart. In fact, I have. Many, many times. Males in space just don't seem to care about clothing. They consider it optional most of the time. The females put their foot down about the dining room, thank goodness, but other than that it's considered perfectly normal to waltz around naked. In the *ludus*? It's expected.

I'll admit, it scandalized me at first, but I thought I'd gotten used to it. Used to it, that is, until a certain someone shifted into humanoid form.

I watched his huge, powerful body fighting with all his might. His muscles strained, sometimes he grunted with effort. There were times he put both hands on the hilt of his sword and swung up and over his head, his muscles flexing under warm tan skin. My mouth was dry as I watched. It's only in the privacy of my own mind that I admit to myself why. Lust. I wanted Bayne in a way I've never wanted another living soul.

His skin was covered in a glistening sheen of sweat. His face was tight, muscles rigid, as he displayed laser focus on the match. It was as if winning that fight was the most important thing in his life.

He thrust and parried. Even when Dax was on the offensive and Bayne had to step backward, he seemed in control of the situation, as if he was simply biding his time, waiting to aggress toward his partner again.

Then Dax spoke to me and Bayne faltered, his concentration obviously derailed. The grace he fought with became awkward, slowed, and then he stopped altogether, setting the tip of his sword on the floor.

Dax stopped his attack, and both males stood stock still, looking at me.

I apologized for interrupting them, set a time to meet with Dax, and hurried out of the *ludus*, my emotions in an turmoil.

For the last month, I'd been in a delusional state, having convinced myself I wasn't interested in Bayne, but as soon as I left the *ludus* and scurried toward my cabin I quit lying to myself. I'm interested. More than interested, I'm obsessed.

I glance into the mirror and look at myself the way I did when I was an adolescent. I remember inspecting myself years ago as my body was changing. Noticing my budding breasts and the subtle changes to the shape of my face. It's with that level of intensity I examine myself now, only this time I'm noticing myself the way Bayne sees me.

An average twenty-five-year-old Earth woman looks back at me. I'd like to believe I'm beautiful. Barring that, I'd like to believe I'm pretty. But I'm just an average woman who wouldn't turn any heads on the street. My eyes are an ordinary shade of brown. My brown hair trails to the middle of my back. I learned to style it well in high school and have always thought it's one of my better features.

The women on the ship have been in space longer than me and have found some decent tools for doing hair and makeup. I've curled the ends of my hair and styled it to frame my face. My makeup is on and my eyes look pretty.

I sway in front of the mirror, making the dress Savannah loaned me float around my thighs. If I'd gone to the best stores in Houston I couldn't have found a dress more flattering than this. She called it a scarf dress. The fabric is a rainbow of colors and the hem has varying lengths. It moves gracefully, pulling the observer's eye to the nip at my waist and the tempting swell of my hips.

I read a book about setting your intentions for something. It was a New Agey thing that proposed that if you set an intention you were more likely to get what you want. It makes sense. You can't get anything if you don't acknowledge your desires and then go after them.

I drop onto the edge of the bed and consider what it is I want, but I don't have to think for long. I want Bayne. It's not just that he's handsome, which is certainly true. He's not just gorgeous, he's sexy. I've brought myself pleasure thinking about him several times since I watched him spar in the *ludus* and realized denying my attraction was futile.

I also admire him. He's taken a shitty situation, worse even than mine, and has swiftly come to terms with it. He's trying to learn everything he can and make a new life for himself.

I don't know if I'm ready to have sex with him, but I'm definitely ready to get to know him.

So my intention for tonight? I want to talk to him, and dance with him. I want to express my interest. I nod my head at myself, still looking into the mirror. I won't let tonight end without Bayne knowing I don't want him banished from my life anymore. I want him to know I'd like . . . more.

When I leave my room and enter the hallway, I realize Bayne might not even be there tonight. What will I do if that happens? Well, I've clearly set my intentions, so I guess I'll just have to knock on his door.

Bayne

As I stride to my room I'm full of purpose. I'm a Skylosian, a warrior—a strong male who knows what he wants. I just need to make it happen. I'll no longer be content to watch Willa from afar. I'm going to woo her.

When I arrive in my room and remove the broadsword from my back scabbard, I happen to see a flash of my movement out of the corner of my eye. I catch a glimpse of myself—huge, muscled adult male, arms bent in the act of pulling the weapon above his head, a serious, almost fierce look on his face.

My world slows down and time stops spinning.

I've been on the Intergalactic Database using my burgeoning reading skills to glean what I can about my homeworld, Skylose. Nothing important has come from all my attempts to trigger memories of my past. But this one glimpse of a ferocious male in the mirror has sliced through the darkness. My past tumbles back to me.

My village was remote. Not all Skylosians were shifters. My pack didn't flaunt our abilities because those who couldn't shift would be envious or hate us. We kept to ourselves and moved farther into the wilderness each year to avoid confrontation.

Now that I've seen other planets and ridden on spaceships, I realize how primitive my planet was. We were warring factions—tribes, really.

I hadn't reached my twentieth birthday the day the marauders came. I had been in the forest with my bow and arrow, hunting little mammals for food. I heard the thunder of hooves as our enemies came, riding six-leggeds.

My tribe, my pack, numbered in the hundreds, including females and younglings. The males on steeds were at least that many, and they had metal swords and the element of surprise, having killed our sentries before the frontal attack.

They surrounded the village, tossed flaming torches at our huts and longhouses, and killed many of our males.

Clutching my weapon, I ran toward the melee to fight. I considered shifting into my canine form but feared they'd kill us all if I revealed the tribe's secret.

I killed a few with my bow and arrows until my quiver was empty, then ran screaming into the fight with nothing but my young fists. By this time, the village was in flames, most of our adult males were dead or dying on the ground, and many of the marauders were taking their fill of our females.

The few males who were left alive were rounded up and held at the point of a sword. I'll never forget the sound their derisive laughter made when they grabbed me and forced me into the shrunken group of my tribesmen.

I remember the bitter taste of my anger which changed to horror as I helplessly watched them violate my mother. My canine growled in unbridled fury, straining to be released. I kept him tightly leashed inside me, believing that if our secret was revealed we would all be killed. My uncle and another male held me back as I screamed in impotent rage.

"Hush," Uncle Tresor said, trying to calm my canine and me. "The only thing you can do now is stay alive. Stay alive by any means possible and live to exact revenge. It's what you've been saved for."

No matter how tightly I squeeze my eyes closed, I can't erase the picture that bombards me. I hear the screams, see the village burning and six-leggeds pawing at the ground. The acrid smell of fire and the tang of the blood is as caustic this moment as it was all those *annums* ago.

All the movement seemed to stop as a contingent of our enemies entered from the rear. Only these weren't Skylosians, I now know these were offworlders, another species who had obviously come from afar. At the time all I could do was gape in speechless shock at these strange beings.

Purple-skinned males approached as the sea of our enemies parted for them. They drove a vehicle the likes of which I'd never seen. It was completely enclosed and hovered off the ground. It was a silent machine.

Five purple males emerged from the fantastical vehicle. Their clothing was made of fabric, not the animal skins Skylosians wore. They surveyed the carnage as if they were looking at a garden filled with beautiful blooms. The sight of my people dead, dying, bleeding, and crying seemed to please them.

I hadn't known of other planets then. Now I understand these were invaders who had chosen to align with Skylose's strongest tribe in order to harvest their enemy and steal males to fight for them. Somehow the offworlders had found out our secret and knew we could shift. Perhaps our enemies had discovered our closely guarded secret and told them in order to spare their own lives. We had been betrayed by our own people. It crushes my soul to this day.

They strode to our group of hearty males and yanked us out of our cluster one by one. They pulled my friend

Grennal out first and demanded he open his mouth to inspect his teeth. When he refused, they pointed a weapon at him and a ray of light beamed from the end of it. Somehow the powerful light killed him.

The purple male in charge barely gave Grennal a glance as he lay charred and unmoving at his feet. "I trust the rest of you will be more cooperative," he ground out.

Uncle Tresor whispered, "Revenge." I followed his guidance and knew it was my duty to live. Knew that one day I would avenge my people. It was a good cause. I could think of none other.

They inspected us one by one, testing our strength and fitness for battle.

Even after being beaten and ravaged, my mother still fought them. While the purple males examined us, the carnage in the village continued.

My heart almost stops beating in my chest as I recall the sight of the marauding chieftain dragging my mother off the ground by her hair and forcing her to stand with several other females in front of the purple males' leader.

When she refused his order to kneel, the chieftain pulled his sword from the scabbard on his back. The purple male accepted the sword, swung it across his body to one shoulder, and then with such swift force I heard it whistle, he sliced through the air, lopping my mother's head from her shoulders as if he was slaughtering livestock.

Every muscle in my body clenches as the scene plays in my mind so slowly I can see every moment. My mother's face, her eyes wide, her scream of terror, the heartbreaking howl of my inner beast filling my head, and my uncle, her brother, placing his hand on my upper arm, biting into it so hard it's as if he's squeezing me this very *minima*.

I can see the exact moment her head was separated from her neck, and then I see no more because my younger self was smart enough to squeeze his eyes closed as the howl in his head was given voice.

The rest of the memory is mostly a blur. My grief was so intense, it was a blessing when I was forced to shift into my canine form and was injected with something that controlled my ability to shift back. Perhaps the decade of darkness was a good thing. It kept me from remembering any of this.

Chapter Five

Bayne

I stood still as a statue for I don't know how long, maybe *minimas*, maybe *hoaras*. When I came to my senses, my broadsword was still in my hand. I hadn't moved.

I let it clatter to the floor, wanting to never hold the abominable thing again. I imagine it will always remind me of that day, of my mother.

I pull off my loincloth and enter the shower, washing my pelt and scrubbing my skin until it feels raw. It's as if I'm trying to wash the blood and smell of fire off my fur and skin, as if it will erase the memory itself. It won't, I know. Nothing will ever make the pictures of what happened that day go away. They're imprinted on my brain.

Although I've pushed those memories out of my mind for a decade, now I sift through them, searching for pictures of those five purple males. I vowed revenge as a young male, then spent a long time in canine form.

Yes, hunt them, kill them. A deep growl reverberates through my body.

I agree, I assure WarDog,

Now I have the means to track them down and kill them. Try as I might, I can't see any of their faces. Perhaps my mind is doing me a kindness by hiding this from me.

The water has long since turned cold, but I keep scrubbing, keep abusing my body with the frigid water, trying to make the horrendous memory recede to where it has hidden all these *annums*. It won't.

At last, I turn off the shower and dry myself, then stand in front of the mirror. I inspect myself. I'm a grown male. I'm strong, powerful. I've fought in the arena, albeit in my shifted form. I vow to find my enemies. Not the males of my homeworld which the Intergalactic Database tells me was almost destroyed by offworlders shortly after I was taken.

No. I vow to myself and to my canine, we will find and destroy those purple males who came in on hovers, provided advanced arms to a neighboring tribe, and incited them to destroy us so the five of them could swoop in and get what they came for—rare fighting stock.

I need to remember who my enemies are—and find them.

In the meantime, I've lost so much. Don't I deserve a female? Don't I deserve the comfort of soft arms? Don't I deserve to sheathe myself in her warm channel and find pleasure there?

Don't I deserve to connect on a deep level with one other being in this galaxy? A female who showed me her compassion many times, albeit only to my canine.

Yes, replies WarDog, *take her, mate her, bite her, make her ours.*

My decision of a few *hoaras* ago still stands. *Patience*, I admonish my enthusiastic beast. *I'm going to pursue the female who has invaded my dreams and consumed every waking thought since I was freed from the prison of my canine form. I have to gain her trust and hopefully her affections will follow.* I hear a chuff of agreement at this plan.

Willa

When I arrive at the dining room, most of the furniture is pushed against the walls. A small spread of party food, as well as ruby-colored punch, is on one of the long tables. I see Bayne talking to Stryker along the back wall. He's in profile, perhaps so he can see everyone who enters.

He doesn't look directly at me, but I know he saw me enter. The corners of my lips lift in a tiny smile because his ear flicked toward me, then he stood a little taller and threw his shoulders back when he sensed my presence.

One thing is certain, that male is handsome. His broad chest is naked except for the black leather sash stretching from one shoulder to the opposite side of his waist. It's sexier than if he was completely bare because it calls attention to every muscle and ripple.

If anything, he's stronger and more muscular than the first time I saw him in his humanoid form. He's wearing a black leather kilt like many of the males on board. It doesn't reach his knees, and accentuates his strong calves.

At first, I thought the pelt on his shoulders was a little Cro-Magnon, but over the last month, watching him at meals and stalking through the halls, I've come to think it accentuates his masculinity, and also his differences.

I'm in space. It's full of aliens. This isn't an Earth male. He's part canine. I appreciate everything about him that underscores our diversity.

I mingle, doing my best to be upbeat and happy, all the while keeping an eye on Bayne. As soon as his conversation with Stryker comes to an end, I'm going to approach him. Carpe Diem! I'm going to seize the day.

"Can you believe it's only been a few *lunars* since we were in that cell on the slave ship together?" Ar'Tok asks. He was a quiet male when we met. Now he's found love and come out of his shell. There's a broad smile on his face—certainly something I never imagined that day we were in an epic space battle and ultimately rescued by the gladiators on this ship.

"I think we've all done a lot of growing since then," I say with a smile. I'm so engrossed in our conversation as we recount all the changes we've experienced, that I take my eye off Bayne for a moment. When I glance toward the back of the room, I don't see him. I hope he hasn't retreated to his cabin.

"Willa, would you like some punch?" It's Bayne. He slipped up on me quietly and is at my elbow, offering me a glass.

"Yes. Thanks." I believe these are the first words we've exchanged since I kicked him out of my cabin. My fingers actually tremble as I accept the glass. He's bigger than I remember, or maybe it's because he's so close. Heat radiates off him. I feel pulled to him as if he's a planet with his own gravity.

I take a sip and realize the fruity red punch packs a kick. Normally not a drinker, I decide tonight would be a good time to treat myself to a glass—or two.

My mind swirls with thoughts and questions. I want to say so many things. What I do, however, is bite my bottom lip with my teeth and feel excitement eddy through my body. Then we both talk at once. I didn't hear what he said.

"Awkward," I admit, then look into those golden eyes for the first time tonight. Maybe I'm crazy, but I think I understand every thought racing through his brain. No, that's not right. But I think I know his feelings. The emotion pouring out of the most beautiful eyes I've ever seen is affection. He's lobbing it at me, propelling at me all the caring and concern I can handle.

Our awkward conversation gets worse before it gets better. I ask him how he's been and he tells me "fine." He asks me what I've been doing and I have nothing to report. What is there to say? I've been helping the other women do the things they're good at because I have no strengths of my own? Or should I admit I've spent a great deal of time regretting kicking him out of my cabin?

It doesn't help that people are watching us. I'm sure we've been the talk of our little ship. He was my constant companion from the day we boarded the *Fool's Errand* until the day he shifted. Thankfully someone turns on some music, but the awkwardness continues, only now it's louder.

He grabs my hand in his huge, warm one. It's like someone plugged me into an electrical current. Something sparks between us. Lust. My gaze flies to his and locks there. I couldn't pull away if I wanted to.

"Come with me?" It's spoken as half request, half command.

I nod, still dumbstruck by the electricity of his touch. When he tugs me toward the exit, I almost pull back. Is he going to yank me toward his cabin with no more preliminaries than this? But I don't resist. I follow.

Instead of heading to the dorm wing, though, I follow him to the end of a different hallway. Grace brought me here once. I loved it, but never took the time to return. She called it the solarium. It's a bullet-shaped room with windows on all sides except the wall with the doorway from which we enter. Even the roof is clear and reminds us we're floating among the stars themselves.

The apprehension I'd experienced when I thought he was dragging me to his room disappears. Every nervous cell in my body stands down. It's silent in here, made even more so when he turns off all the lights. The room is only illuminated by the red of the running lights on the rear exterior of the ship.

We still haven't spoken one substantive word in over a month. He leads me to a comfy couch at the back of the room. We sit side by side and gaze out at the stars.

"Beautiful," I say on a sigh.

"I like it here," he responds.

At times I feel his gaze on me, but mostly we just watch the black velvet canvas strewn with diamonds. That's what it seems like to me. The stars twinkle like gemstones. There's a blue and purple nebula off to our right reminding us just how vast the universe is.

Reaching over, he uses one finger to lift my chin and tip my head toward him. I don't understand how, but in this dim light, his golden eyes swirl with an otherworldly glow.

"Are you still mad at me?" he asks, cocking his head in the manner I find so adorable.

"I never—" I protest, but cut myself off. I didn't set honesty as my intention earlier, but I should have. "I know I acted mad, Bayne, but it was driven by shame."

"I've spoken with several females on board. I never breathed a word you would consider private, but I asked about the situation in general. They all agreed it would be hard to tolerate. Maddie said it would be like having a suitor read your diary before a first date. I had no idea what a diary or a first date was but she said it would put the female at a distinct disadvantage. I apologize."

"But you didn't do anything wrong." I cup his cheek with my palm as I inspect him. Prominent cheekbones, furred pelt, canines that peek out when he says certain letters, and those gorgeous eyes.

"Do you really believe that?" he asks, penetrating me with his gaze.

"Now I do. It took me a while."

"I've learned a lot since we talked last." He mirrors me, his calloused palm on my cheek. I hold his hand close to me so he can't slip away.

"Like what"

"A little cooking, baking, and music-making. A moment of star-charting—I will not make a habit of that, I found it a terrible combination of difficult and boring. A lot of fighting. Weapons, shooting, and swordplay. When to attack, when to retreat. What arms work best for what type of adversary. Many other things. I had a lot to catch up on."

"Yes, you did. Do you feel you've caught up?"

"No. Not nearly. But I'm certain I will. One thing I never learned the answer to, though."

"What's that?"

By the heated look on his face, I know this is going to be important. I also know I stepped into a trap.

"After how many *hoaras* is it not considered rude to ask a female to have sex*?*"

My gaze has never left his, but I try to pierce deeper, as if things are written there that hold all the answers.

That's when he does it. He hits me with a thousand-watt smile. It gives me all the information I need. He was serious! But he's tempered it with humor. He's right, he *has* learned a lot in the last month.

"I'll need a computer," I tell him seriously, then give him my own megawatt smile. "There are some high-level calculations I'll need to make. And," I pet his cheek again, "I'd really have to like the guy."

"So tell me, Willa. What would a *guy* have to do for you to *really like* him?"

"Well," I tip my head and look up at the ceiling, "he'd have to take me to a solarium."

"Yes?"

"And he'd have to look at me with affection."

"Yes?"

"And he'd have to tell me about his life . . . over time of course, not all at once."

"Yes?"

"And he'd dance with me."

"So have I taken you to a solarium?"

"Yes."

"And do I look at you with affection?"

"Oh yes. I see that now." I lean a bit closer, part my lips, and silently will him to kiss me.

"And could I make a date with you to tell you about my life? There's not much to tell, though. I remember almost nothing." His gaze flashes to the floor for a moment.

"I'd like to make a date with you," I say, making sure I fan him with my breath, a gentle reminder that my lips are parted and I'm waiting for our first kiss.

"And can I ask you to dance, Willa?"

Perhaps I'll have to make the first move for the kiss. I think I made the poor guy wary.

"I'd love to dance with you, Bayne."

He stands with a powerful grace I've noticed many times from afar and he pulls me from my seat. I thought he'd escort me back to the dining room where there are other people, and, more importantly, music. But he pulls me close, tucks me against him, and hums.

It's like no music I've ever heard. Perhaps it's Skylosian. Maybe it's something he just composed. It doesn't matter. As far as I'm concerned it doesn't even have to be music. I'm in his arms!

One warm palm lodges at the small of my back, the other cups the nape of my neck. He tugs my pelvis next to his and leads me with the slightest pressure. All the skills I observed in the *ludus*—his ability to move with lightning speed, his agility, his grace—they're just as at home on the dance floor as in the gym.

"You're an amazing dancer." I can't help it. The words just popped out.

"Really?" But he's not interested in words right now, and truth be told, neither am I. He dips his head and puts his mouth to my ear. "I missed you, Willa. I'd grown accustomed to your presence. We barely went an *hoara* without you touching me, petting me. WarDog liked that. I would too."

Bayne

Was that too forward? It will take a while to get the hang of this humanoid form, these humanoid interactions. But my hands on her body don't feel anger radiating off her. Leaning to look at her, I see the tiniest smile on her pink lips. Perhaps the time we spent apart was worth it.

My cock is hard, pulsing against her abdomen. She has to feel it. It's not subtle. She doesn't push me away, though, she presses me closer, her tiny hands on the bare skin at the small of my back.

The smell of the arousal she denies is perfuming the air, but I'm not stupid. I won't mention it. WarDog wants to sniff, but I make him do it on soft breaths. It soothes him.

My lips are at her ear, humming softly. It's a folk tune of my people. I don't know why it came to mind just now. I hadn't remembered it until it started to flow out of my mouth. Perhaps it was triggered by the thunderous cavalcade of memories I had in my room earlier. I push those away. They have no place with me here, now.

Although I need to wait to ask to share pleasure, I don't think I'll ask for the kiss. My hunch is it will be better if I just take it.

I quit humming and press my lips to the spot on her neck behind her ear.

"Mmm," she responds.

That's a clear message.

She likes us, WarDog whispers. *Mate her.*

Hopefully soon, I respond.

Gentle kisses follow and receive no rebuke, so my tongue cuts a swath along her hairline. She breathes in on a little gasp, so I forge ahead with kisses and nips punctuated by little tracings of my tongue. She likes those the best, so I dispense them sparingly.

Her muscles are looser than when we started. She's enjoying this. I'll take it as tacit permission until she rescinds it. Nibbling along her jawline with my blunt front teeth, I decide to take a chance.

I nip her with the sharp tips of my canine teeth. Maybe it's fully my decision, or maybe the canine inside me incited me to do it. He really wants me to bite her, to mark her as ours. *Down boy,* I command with a warning to my voice. *We can't rush her.*

She gasps. It's a soft, quiet sound, but I pull back. The last thing I want to do is hear the word 'no' escape her lips.

I don't, though. Instead, she tips her head, exposing the vulnerable column of her neck to me, a silent request for more.

My cock kicks in excitement and my fingers curl more tightly into her flesh. I scrape a line with one sharp fang along the gentle curve of her jaw. Her eyelids flutter closed and her breathing comes in little pants. The scent of her arousal teases my nose.

I consider asking for a proper kiss, then dismiss the thought and take it. My lips land softly at first, then when I hear no protests, I slant my lips against hers and take what I want, like a marauding army. WarDog thumps his tail in approval as he scoots closer.

Chapter Six

Willa

I've imagined this for so long. First with the nameless huntsman in my dreams, and later with Bayne. He's kissing me. I'm so excited it feels like too much work to drag air into my lungs. I just want to kiss and be kissed until the end of time.

He's stroking my tongue with his. I opened to him the moment his lips claimed mine. I don't want him to wonder, even for a second if he has an invitation. To underscore my welcome, I pull away just long enough to whisper his name. "Bayne."

He pauses for a moment. When I open my eyes to see what the problem is, I see his questing eyes. He's making sure my saying his name was a request and not a rebuke.

"More kisses," I urge as I allow my lids to flutter closed and give over all control to him. Much to my enjoyment, he seizes the control I ceded and penetrates deeper into the hidden cavern of my mouth.

His tongue is slightly sweet and very hot. It tickles and burns and sets my world on fire. I can't think of anything except the word 'more'. My hands are firmly lodged on his neck, under his long hair, enjoying the feel of the fur pelt covering his shoulders. My fingers burrow down to the hot skin underneath—it's warm and soft.

My nipples prick beneath the fabric of my dress as they drag against his bare chest. I want him. I've never been so comfortable with a male before, and certainly never wanted one with the powerful desperation I do now.

Our kisses aren't quiet. They're punctuated with wet smacks and deep sighs of pleasure. His taste is an interesting combination of sweet and spicy. I feel compelled to inform him of this.

"You taste so good," I tell him eloquently.

He doesn't answer, simply strokes my tongue and lodges his hands at my waist.

"I've wanted to do this since that day I shifted on Aeon II," he says.

"I was so embarrassed."

"That's over now, but if we stay here any longer, I think I'll make you unhappy again." He pulls away, panting, his eyes roaming my face as if he can't believe we're here in this intimate embrace.

"No. Nothing you're doing is making me unhappy," I tell him, trying to hide the whine from my voice. I want to keep kissing.

"Our first coupling should be perfect, and if we don't leave, it will be here. We should join the others. Dancing should be accompanied by music, don't you think?"

He's right. This isn't the right time or place.

He grabs my hand and pulls me to the doorway.

"You look beautiful tonight, Willa. Like a picture."

The way he's looking at me, I wish I could capture it for eternity. The golden swirls in his eyes, the affection, the . . . lust. I should bottle this moment.

He grabs my hand and stalks to the doorway like a male on a mission. I scurry to keep up with his long strides and follow toward the dining room where lively music is playing.

These people have become my friends—both of our friends. Every eye in the room is trained on us upon our return. They've been secretly and not so secretly hoping Bayne and I would patch up our relationship after our quarrel. Looking at my small hand clutched in his big one, I guess it's no secret that things have changed between us.

Aerie gives me a close-lipped smile, and I see Stryker nod approvingly at Bayne. I love being on this ship. It's like the best and worst of a large family. Some of them can be intrusive, maybe even bossy, but you know every single one of them has your best interests at heart.

Aerie and her mate Beast are here for the dance from the *Devil's Playground*. Wow, Beast's dancing is erotic as sin. Aerie is totally enraptured. Huh...never would have guessed the big guy had it in him.

Bayne pulls me to the back corner and dances. I don't know the first thing about his home planet, or his people, but watching him dance I wonder if they were primitive. There's something about the way his hips sway and his feet pound that I can imagine him performing these same actions around a flickering bonfire.

At first, I'm shy and just sway my hips in time with the music. Bayne doesn't judge, he just keeps dancing, allowing the music to carry him away. I catch my reflection in the metal wall and notice the juxtaposition of our images.

His wild gyrations pulse with immediacy. At times he throws his head back in the sheer exuberance of the moment. My staid little two-step doesn't do him justice.

I focus on the hem of my scarf dress as it gently sways. Setting my goal to make it swing, I snap my hips from side-to-side. I like the way the fabric moves. Keeping my gaze away from the reflection of my face, knowing I'd be embarrassed, I just focus on the hem. When it's moving more wildly, I pay attention to the feelings in my body.

It feels good to shake my hips in time with the music, to feel the pulsing beat and allow my torso and limbs to dive in and experience it. It's as if I'm savoring music for the first time. I immerse myself even deeper, allowing my shoulders into the mix. Then my head, as it dips front to back and side to side.

I'm fully in the music for the first time in my life. When I glance at my reflection I see the hem of my dress twirling and floating, giving glimpses of calves and knees and even a flash of my thighs.

The male in the reflection looks like he belongs with me. We're both gyrating primitively to the pounding beat. I'm having fun! And my body is fully alive.

I toss my head back and laugh, my lips turned up in a happy smile. For the first time since we entered the dining room, I look comfortably into Bayne's eyes.

"We look good together," he says, his heated gaze on me, that golden gaze flicking from my head to my toes and back again.

I move close to him, throw my arms around his furred shoulders, and place my lips next to his ear. "Indeed."

Was Grace watching? She's disc jockeying tonight, and she chose this moment to change from the hammering beat of this fast song to a slow ballad she found somewhere on the Intergalactic Database.

Bayne slips his arms around me, his hands resting on my hips, and tugs me closer. Everything is different than it was a moment ago. From frenzied movement, hips thrusting, head bobbing, to melting into my partner's embrace.

My mind takes a snapshot of every detail of this moment. I love the feel of my fingers in Bayne's pelt. It's an auburn ruff that matches his hair and covers his shoulders and upper back. The hair is soft, just like WarDog's. If someone had described this to me back on Earth it probably would have sounded awful, but here, now, on Bayne, it's wonderful.

It's soft and makes the skin underneath it even warmer than the rest of his body. It enhances his masculinity and the fact that he's alien. I like that he's not like anyone I dated before. He's different. Sexier.

My hands trail lower, skimming over the black leather sash crossing his back so they can touch his warm exposed skin. There's something so compelling about his soft skin covering hard muscles below. My palms lodge respectfully at his waist, unwilling to violate the boundary of his kilt.

His hands, though, aren't being quite so respectful. They're roaming wildly up and down my back. From the nape of my neck and my shoulders to my waist, then making little forays lower. When I don't protest, they rise to my shoulder blades, then slide down my back and lodge even lower each time.

Now his palms are resting on the globes of my ass. Not tight, mind you. Not clenching, but soft, like a whisper. Their heat seeps through, and knowing they're so close to my private parts sets my world on fire.

He tugs me to him, and I feel his erection even though it's covered by the stiff leather of his kilt. One large palm grips my ass and drags me closer while the other cups the nape of my neck and pulls me toward him so he can own my mouth.

This kiss is nothing like what we shared in the solarium. Perhaps he was holding back there because there were no chaperones—no external constraints. Here he knows he can't tear off my clothes and sheathe himself in me, so he can play with fire.

And play with fire he does. He's kissing me with fervor, his lips slanting down on mine, savoring the feeling, tasting me from all angles. He's holding nothing back, making soft moaning sounds from the back of his throat.

His tongue flicks against the seam of my mouth and I open to him expectantly. Welcoming him inside me. My mind flashes me a picture of how I'll welcome him inside me in other ways, hopefully later tonight.

Desire slams into me. It strikes in my belly, then rips through me like wildfire, pricking the tips of my breasts, igniting in my pelvis, and creating an epicenter in my clit.

My entire body is sensitized after coming online during our wild, primitive dance. Now my little bundle of nerves is pounding, demanding, and announcing its need by pulsing. My channel quivers.

Bayne sniffs. It's just one quick intake of breath. I imagine the canine inside him couldn't help himself. I'm certain he smells my need. Although I denied it in the past, I'm certain there's no denying it now. In fact, I have no desire to.

I double down. Instead of disavowing it, I press my lips to his canine-shaped ear and whisper, "I want you, Bayne."

He slides his hands so they're each cupping one of my ass cheeks and easily lifts me off the floor, pulling me against him so his hard cock presses against my neediest spot. He doesn't stop there, lifting me up and down in tiny pulses, massaging me in full view of everyone in the room.

Instead of looking around, guaranteeing my mortification, I close my eyes and delve into the feeling of desire snaking through every cell in my body.

He slowly slides me down until my feet touch the floor again, then lodges one hand at my waist, one between my shoulder blades, and continues our dance.

"You're a naughty male." My words scold, but there's no censure in my voice.

"I was just thinking the same thing about you." He flashes me a smile full of sharp, white teeth. Instead of frightening me, they spark a zing of lust through my body.

We continue dancing, through fast tempos and slow ballads. Every minute that passes ratchets up my desire. Although my hands were intimately acquainted with his canine form, I'd petted him for months, we've only touched his humanoid form for a few hours.

On this dance floor, he's touched me almost everywhere—except the few square inches that matter. My body wants him. No. My body is desperate for him.

Finally, the first couple leaves the room, giving us an excuse to follow.

"Join me, Bayne? Join me in my room?" I gaze into those swirling golden eyes.

"You're sure you want this? You're ready? We can wait."

I wonder how hard it must be for him to have offered that. He's been rock hard for hours, and the fact that there's a primitive canine inside him must be another yearning he needs to control.

"No." I shake my head. "No more waiting." If he doesn't leave with me soon, I'm going to tear off that kilt and mount him on the dance floor.

He pulls me toward Maddie the cook and thanks her for the delicious spread she prepared, although neither of us tasted a morsel. Then he approaches Grace and praises her for the music she found to entertain us.

Now he grips my small hand in his large one and drags me toward the doorway and down the hall. What started out as a swift walk has turned into a jog until we arrive at my door. I slap my hand on the palm plate and we slip inside before the door fully opens, as if the entire adventure had been choreographed.

We giggle for a moment, thrilled with our little escapade, then it's silent in our little room.

"Has it been enough *hoaras*?" he asks, his gorgeous face serious, as if he doesn't want to break my rules.

I nod, a shy smile on my face. I don't know how this handsome male could be any more beautiful, but the blend of relief and desire on his face makes me want him even more.

It suddenly occurs to me that I wouldn't have made a good girl scout. I'm not prepared. "I hadn't expected this, Bayne. I'm not on any protection."

After having been in canine form for the last decade, it takes him a moment to comprehend my meaning.

"We can't . . .?" His eyes dip to the 'v' between my legs then back to my face.

"There are many things we *can* do. But I don't want to make a baby."

A shadow crosses his face. I don't know if it's in response to my rejection or if perhaps he doesn't understand what I'm saying. If he lived on a primitive planet, perhaps he doesn't know how babies are made. Is that even possible?

"The many things we can do, Willa, they would include this?" he asks, a wicked smile on his face as he slides his palms across my breasts, over the fabric. Even with layers of clothes in the way, the heat of his skin and the intimacy of his touch pricks my nipples. I magically feel a corresponding zing in my nethers.

"They would," I answer solemnly.

"And these many things, they would include this?" He tilts his head as the flat of his palm slips between my legs, the heel of his hand pressing on my clit.

After I suck in a sharp intake of breath, I answer, "They would."

"And my mouth, Willa? Could my mouth explore anywhere it wants?"

"Absolutely, Bayne."

"And would there be any prohibitions against bringing you pleasure? I wouldn't want to violate any rules."

"No. No prohibitions against that." I relieve him of the need to ask the next question by offering, "As there are no prohibitions against my mouth exploring or bringing *you* pleasure."

"I've dreamed of that, Willa. All those things," his tone is urgent and sweet and sexy—a potent combination.

I love his direct innocence and decide to honor him with mine, even though it's not as easy for me. "I've dreamed of it too, Bayne."

After its incursion between my legs, his hand has been curled at his side. Six inches separate us, although it feels like a mile.

The hum of the motors is the only sound in the cabin. I feel the gentle vibration through the soles of my feet. It's just Bayne and me, both standing still, shoulders stiff, gazing into each other's eyes. I feel as if I'm waiting for the starter's pistol.

Bam. It's almost as if we both hear it. He erases the distance between us, places his hands on my waist, and drags my body against his. His kiss is a hard possession, speaking volumes of need and desire. My response is just as clear as I kiss him back with no hesitation, no reservations.

We're no longer in the dining room with every soul on board watching. We're alone in this room, having already agreed to our plan of action. I kick off my shoes, lift my leg, and surround him with it. My heel against the back of his thigh, I pull him closer so I can feel the hard ridge of his cock between the lee of my thighs.

Moaning with pleasure, I grind against him, my eyes flashing open at the ferocity of my desire and my lack of restraint. He takes my cue and presses me closer, rubbing against me. He may be the canine, but I feel like a bitch in heat.

He drags his mouth from mine long enough to pull my dress over my head. I feel shy for a moment, then embarrassed when I remember that he's seen me naked hundreds of times. I had put that out of my mind.

"You're beautiful, Willa," his voice is deep and full of passion. No matter what I see when I look at myself in the mirror, I far prefer the affirmation that's in his eyes. When he says I'm beautiful, I have no doubt he means it.

He rips my bra over my head and tosses it onto the floor to join the dress. When his eyes flick to the patch of fabric covering my sex, I move to drag it over my hips. He shakes his head and steps even closer.

His palms start at my shoulders, skimming downward along my upper arms, forearms and circling my wrists. They travel to my waist, his thumbs hooking my panties, and then glide down as he kneels in front of me.

Both Bayne and my panties are now at my feet. He looks up at me like a knight pledging fealty to his queen.

"Granted," I say, not even sure what I mean, just giving him permission to do whatever he wants from here on out.

His mouth is at my navel of all places. Certainly not what I've been dreaming of, but when the tip of his tongue invades that space, I must admit it's more erotic than I ever dreamed. Then his teeth score a line to the seam of my leg.

He springs to his feet and lifts me in one fluid motion. After setting me on the edge of my bed, he goes down on his knees, splits me wide, and dips his tongue into my center.

For a moment, I wish for more foreplay, then realize the last two hours have been foreplay. No, the last month has been as I've watched him stalk around the ship wearing nothing more than a scrap of fabric around his sex.

I'm lying on my back, the soles of my feet on the edge of the bed where he placed them. His tongue thrusts into me, licking and piercing and devouring me. His thumbs have pulled apart my outer lips, his fingers surround my clit, titillating my bundle of nerves but not touching. The tip of his tongue slides along my slick slit on a slow journey to the little bud that is desperate with desire.

My fingers glide through his silky hair and lodge on his furred shoulders as I prepare to hang on for the ride. His strong hands grip my hips as if he has the need to hold me in place although the last thing on my mind is any desire to wiggle out of his grasp.

"Oh!" escapes my mouth at the exquisite pleasure of his tongue. At times it's almost delicate as it licks and swipes. Then he picks up my subtle cues as I press closer, and he applies more pressure to the perfect spot.

An orgasm sneaks up on me. I didn't even feel it build as my muscles spasm. It's one of those events you're not even sure is a climax, with a few half-hearted spasms that hardly give you release—they just leave you wanting more.

Bayne's beautiful head lifts to inspect me, a quizzical look on his face, his head tipped, brow slightly lowered. The embarrassing awareness comes barreling at me that he's seen me orgasm before, and this was nothing like what he spied as a furry creature.

What he watched from the side of my bed was usually frenzied self-pleasuring of the one-and-done variety designed to get me off and then get on with my day or go to sleep. Does he think his work here is done?

"More." I don't know how my voice is breathy and demanding at the same time.

He grins at me, making no effort to hide his long, sharp teeth, then removes his clothes before he returns to his task. This time he's less goal-driven. He nuzzles me with his nose, gives me the most careful nips with canine teeth, and teases me until my fingers grip his pelt.

My head whips back and forth on the pillow as I clutch him, moaning. I love looking at his auburn head bobbing between my legs, feeling the hard rasp of his fingers at my hips, and that talented, dedicated tongue providing me endless pleasure.

This time when my climax builds, there's no doubt it's going to be a real one. My thighs quiver as I press against his tongue even harder, straining to reach the pinnacle. When his hand slips up my thigh, awakening every nerve ending along the way, I'm panting—so close.

"Yes!" One hundred percent of my focus is on that hand, hoping it will lodge in my hot, waiting channel.

One thick finger slides inside me, giving my waiting muscles something to clamp onto. I release at that moment with a long, low keen of pleasure. The spasm lingers for glorious moments as my pelvis arches off the bed and my fingers tighten in his fur.

The orgasm went on so long, the muscles in my belly feel tender. I almost feel too spent to pull him up to lie with me.

His lips bestow affectionate kisses to me, dotting my face with the sweetest little smacks. I smell myself on him. It's intimate.

"That was amazing," I say after dragging my lids open so I can look into his beautiful, swirling golden eyes.

His answer is a low growl that is as far from aggressive as a sound can be. It's rough and masculine and appreciative.

"Highest praises to you, Sir."

He nips me with his blunt front teeth, then scrapes one sharp canine down the curve of my jawline.

After pulling me close so we're both lying on our hips, he holds me in his arms, somehow rocking me a bit. I feel safer than I've felt in a long time, and allow myself to sink into the feeling.

"So that's what you meant when you offered to ease me? I don't know what I was thinking when I refused," I joke, but it's also meant as an apology.

"We'll make up for it now," he promises. "The males talk about their females constantly. They say Earth females are capable of endless pleasure. I'd like to experiment—I wonder what they mean by endless?"

He laughs, but I think he's serious. He won't get any complaints from me.

"And you, Bayne? Are you ready for *your* pleasure?"

A shadow of sadness flits across his face, then he hides it with a smile as he says, "Always."

I can't read his mind, but for a moment I remember how long he was in canine form, and how little pleasure he's had in his life. This thought just makes me want to give him more of it.

With both palms, I push him onto his back, taking a moment to enjoy the contrast of the smooth skin on his chest as opposed to the thick fur on his shoulders. I straddle his waist, feeling his hard cock standing tall, straining along the seam of my ass.

"Fast or slow, Bayne? Want me to make you desperate, or are you already there?"

"I've waited a long time for this." His jaw is tight, his nostrils flared, and every muscle in his body is poised to explode.

"I want to make you feel so good, Bayne," I say with a shy smile.

I lean forward, plant one perfect close-lipped kiss on his mouth, then kiss a trail to his chin, down his throat, between his pecs, over sculpted abs, and through his happy trail until I'm face-to-face with his cock.

It's a gorgeous cock, as these things go, and accentuates the fact that he's an alien. It's thick, hard, and long, a lighter golden color than his skin, and has a plump head that is already weeping one luminous milky bead of pre-cum which I swipe with my tongue. It has a spicy, almost cinnamon tang to it.

The most distinguishing feature, though, is that instead of being a cylinder, it's more like three balls stacked on top of each other. The one at the base is the thickest, the middle slightly less so, and the top is more the size of a human male.

For a moment I wonder how it will fit when the time comes, then I set another intention, which is to embrace whatever comes—which should be Bayne in a few minutes.

I ring the flat of my tongue around his head and use my tongue tip to explore the underside of his crown. His vigorous hip upthrust tells me I'm on the right track. A few more laps around the head of his cock, and his long fingers lodge in my hair.

Somehow I know he's using all his restraint to keep from jamming me down onto his cock. I'll save him the trouble.

Opening wide, I moan with pleasure as I welcome him into the warmth of my mouth. He moans in response, his fingers tightening in my hair. Reaching between his legs, I hold the weight of his balls in my palm as I ease myself as far as I can down his shaft until my lips are in the hollow between the first and second bulb.

After several trips up and down, his cock thoroughly wet from my saliva, I get to work bobbing up and down, my tongue licking as I go. It's easy to be generous with Bayne. Not only was he equally generous to me, but giving him pleasure is as exciting as receiving it.

I push myself further and get halfway down the second bulge, then use my tongue to swipe further. The indent between the two bulbs is extra sensitive—he moans then snarls. The sound is so passionate I find it sexy.

I can tell he's close, his hips are making micro-thrusts. I know he's trying not to choke or overwhelm me, it's just that this must feel incredible to him. I want to taste him, but at the last minute, he forcefully pulls me off of him and releases toward the side of the bed, grunting in ecstasy, and finishing with a satisfied growl.

Lifting me under my arms, he pulls me to lie on his chest and pets my head as he murmurs and kisses my temple.

"Good?" Silly question. The orgasm, grunt, and growl were pretty self-explanatory.

"Better than my fantasies, and those were pretty good." He kisses me again.

"Next time I want to taste you," I say, unable to drag my gaze from his.

He tilts his head to inspect my face, not certain he believes me, but doesn't answer. If he was like most men, this would be his cue to roll over and snore, but he leaps out of bed, grabs a towel and cleans up, then slides into bed and snuggles me.

I don't know where our relationship is going, but I certainly like where we are.

Chapter Seven

Bayne

I wake with Willa wrapped in my arms. I've woken close to her many times since I met her, but it was always when I was in canine form.

Yes, WarDog sighs with contentment, *her touch, her pats, her cuddles, her kisses, we were seldom apart.* I feel a sudden surge of jealousy and resentment which I quickly suppress.

Since I've been walking on two legs again, I dreamed of sweet Willa in my arms, and here we are. My arm is slung tightly around her waist, her head resting on the fur of my shoulder and her little hand splayed out on my chest as if she's seeking my heat. A small smile plays at the corners of her mouth. My lips tip into an easy smile knowing I make her happy even in sleep.

Nibbling at her mouth, I wake her. I get the privilege of seeing her first true smile of the morning.

"Bayne," her grin stretches wider when she realizes she's in bed with me. "I'm so glad last night wasn't just a dream. You're here, and you're hot." One eyebrow raises as if she just told a dirty joke.

I kiss her playfully, but when she kisses me back there's nothing playful about it. Soon our tongues are exploring each other, then my head bends to her breast and she rolls onto her back in open invitation. I try to replay the events of last night, but she has other ideas.

She climbs on top of me, her knees above my shoulders as she faces my feet, and plays with my already hard cock. Although I want to pay attention to what my sweet

Willa is doing to me, her bottom is less than a hand's breadth from my face. My slow morning brain finally wises up to the obvious invitation, and within a moment we're pleasuring each other at the same time. This must be one of the things the other males boasted about when they talked of the endless pleasure Earth females loved to give and receive.

When we're both spent and panting, our heads finally near each other on the pillows again, Captain Zar's voice booms over the comm.

"Males and females. I'm sorry to interrupt, but I've arranged with Captain Beast of the *Devil's Playground* to meet today. His crew will be boarding within the *hoara*. When that is complete, the crew of both ships will meet in the dining room. I'll comm to tell you when to join us."

I wonder if Beast knows I'm no longer in canine form. Several months ago, Beast, Aerie, another gladiator named Ar'Tok, Willa, and I were in a holding cell on a slave ship bound for auction.

The moment Willa saw me I could sense her fear. Now that my thinking is clearer it's obvious why. My canine form was huge, and my long, sharp teeth as well as my collar's four-inch metal spikes must have been intimidating.

In order to calm her, I crawled to her on my belly, then nudged her hand with my nose. She instantly relaxed and began to pet me. From that first moment, we were inseparable—until I changed into my two-legged form.

Since then Ar'Tok mated Star, a human female he rescued from a malfunctioning satellite, and Beast and Aerie mated. We appropriated the slave ship and Beast, a natural leader, was elected captain. Along the way, we rescued more gladiators, most of whom are on his ship, the *Devil's Playground*. I saw him at the dance last night but the chemistry between him and Aerie was so hot I doubt he was aware of anyone other than her.

Something big must be about to happen if the two ships have converged and we're having a meeting of all hands.

"Think we have time for a bit more fun before we jump in the shower?" Willa asks, her face no longer the picture of innocence it was before. She looks wanton and sexy. How could I not oblige?

We're both clean and dressed when Zar's next announcement intrudes. Before we leave the room, Willa asks, "Are we . . .?"

Because of the animal inside me, my intuition is keen, but even with all of that, I have no idea what she's asking. When I cock my head in question, my ears flicking, she clarifies.

"Do you want to wait until we've been together longer before we let everyone know we're together? A couple?"

"Are you asking me to sneak to my cabin and pretend I didn't spend the night taking you to the heights of pleasure?" My stomach clenches. I didn't realize the connection that felt so real to me might mean nothing to her. "Is that what you want?"

"No. I just wondered if you might not want everyone to know."

"I'm proud to be with you, Willa. I'll announce it on the Intergalactic Database if you'd like."

She laughs. "I don't think you have to go that far. I'll just skip over 'It's Complicated' and go straight to 'In A Relationship' on my Facebook Status." She laughs again and grabs my hand. I have no idea what she meant, but she doesn't want to hide the fact that we pleasured each other all night and half the morning.

The hallway is filled with people filing toward the dining room. Some of their relationships baffle me. Maddie and Stryker, for example. Sometimes they sleep together, sometimes they stay in separate rooms. Earth females can be complicated.

As we move to take our seats, Beast approaches me. He's called a Pinnacle fighter, one of the ten top gladiators in the galaxy. The five rings on the bridge of his nose signify that fact. I've watched him fight; he's a force to be reckoned with.

You'd never know it now, though. He has a pleasant smile on his face and reaches to slap my upper arm in camaraderie.

"Aerie told me of your transformation; I had no idea," he tells me seriously. "I thought you were canine. If I'd known, I would have done everything in my power to help you turn back into your humanoid form."

"I understand," I assure him. He clasps my forearm in formal greeting as I clasp his. "I'm Bayne."

"I'm glad to meet you, Bayne. You have a standing invitation to move to my ship if you'd like. You and your female," he nods happily at Willa.

"Thanks."

We take our seats after he walks away.

"I guess the word's out," Willa says as she grabs my hand and pulls it to the top of the table. It's an announcement in case anyone in the room missed it. It makes me feel proud and accepted.

"Welcome all," Zar says, a handful of paper notes clutched in his hand. "I believe you all know each other, although WarDog has changed his form. On two legs we call him Bayne."

A few of the gladiators from the *Devil's Playground* nod and say hello from across the room.

"We have serious business to discuss. As you know, I'm the captain in day-to-day matters and if things are urgent. I thank you again for the faith you've put in me by voting me captain. My counterpart, Beast, functions the same way on the *Playground*. In long-term matters, we function as what the Earth females call a democracy.

"I will try to get everyone up to speed so you can all make informed decisions in the vote we'll be having later today. While you all have time to think about the weighty matters at hand, our fabulous chef, Maddie has thrown together a celebratory feast.

"Before we discuss matters of war, let's remember all the things we have to celebrate. There are no slaves on board these ships. Many of us have found loving mates and those that haven't have found a tribe of our own where we are cared for and respected."

It is gladiator custom to pound a foot in appreciation, which they do while the females clap. I pound my foot, glad to have only two of them.

"Back to the business at hand. For those of you who don't know, many of us from the original ship were owned by the MarZan cartel. We fought our captors and overthrew the ship. That was about an *annum* ago. Since then MarZan has been pursuing us. According to them, we're still their property.

"At times we've evaded them for days or weeks, once even a *lunar*, but they are always on the hunt. These are not nice people. They don't treat their enemies well.

"We've made friends with a band of pirates on the *Ataraxia*. When we recently met up with them, they informed us one of their males, Sextus, the big blue Cerulean, was in the process of being flayed alive when he fought back and wounded the leader of the cartel, Daneur Khour.

"Although Khour's face was destroyed by Frain acid, he has not become weaker. In fact, over the last *lunar* he has redoubled his efforts to find us."

I reach around Willa's waist and snug her to me. I wish I could allay her fears; she looks terrified.

"Beast and I have been talking. We believe it's time to quit this game. We're fighters, gladiators, warriors. We don't like being prey. I suggest it's time to quit running and become the aggressors.

"We aren't as numerous as the cartel, but we have good, strong males, smart females, a fighting spirit, and the will to take back our own power and quit cowering and hiding in fear.

"Our intel suggests Khour has moved from his retreat on Ortheon to his compound on Fairea. Although it will be hard to penetrate, we have more males than he has guards. I believe if we put our heads together we can come up with a plan to vanquish him."

"Fairea," Brianna breathes, "one of my mates almost died last time we were there. It's not my favorite planet."

"The terrorist attack was a one-time thing. There have been no more incidents of that nature," Zar says.

"Even if we kill him, wouldn't his second-in-command just take his place?" Dax asks. He's a huge male who spars with me often. I count him as a friend. He's vowed not to fight in the gladiator ring again. For a mountain of a man, he has the spirit of an artist.

"Good question," Beast answers. "He very well may, but we believe Khour has made this personal. Hopefully, whoever takes his place won't be as obsessed with pursuing us as Khour is, especially after we attack Khour's compound and kill a contingent of his males."

More questions are asked, more whispering occurs at the dining room tables next to us, and people begin to mull this over.

"I'll let you think about this until we reconvene at 1500. Here's a vid of our adversary. They say Sextus ruined his face, but the only picture we have is from his younger days, before he rose in the ranks of the cartel, when he was just a foot soldier who reaped conscripts from more primitive planets."

There are vid screens on every wall of the dining hall except the one with the large three-dimensional wooden sculpture Dax carved. It shows a peaceful hillside covered with flowers. He told me he'd teach me how to carve soon. I wonder if I could ever make anything half as beautiful as that.

The vid screens come to life and show a picture of a lavender male. I'm certain I quit breathing as my body turns to stone. On every screen in the room is a picture of the male who separated my mother's head from her body in front of my young eyes. He's the male responsible for stealing me from my planet and enslaving me in my canine form.

When I finally begin breathing again, the feeling of hatred overwhelms me. My fists clench as heat boils through my body. I taste blood and realize my fangs have bitten into my lower lip. Before I start crunching bones, I yank my hand out of Willa's and lodge it in my lap.

Zar answers a few more questions, but that only serves as background noise as my mind catapults me back to that terrible day. I'd been unable to see details when my memories assaulted me before. I certainly see them clearly now.

He allowed a warring tribe of Skylosians to do his dirty work. They'd sacked the village, set it on fire, and rounded most of us up. When he pulled up in his hover, much of the slaughter was over.

I was still a teen, not yet twenty *annums* old, and had recently grown taller and stronger. Everyone in the village had remarked on how I was going to be a big male like my father had been. Sadly, my growth spurt would serve the cartel's purposes well.

My eyes were riveted on the hover as it glided over the ground without touching it. We were a primitive planet, none of us had seen anything like it. The first things that emerged were shiny black boots, then Khour unfolded himself to his full height and strode to our band of males. We'd been herded into a small group at the point of knives and swords. Many of those who fought were slaughtered.

Just as Khour and four others of his purple race arrived, the remaining females were dragged to where the males had been gathered. My mother was among them. I'll never forget her proud bearing even as the others cowered and wailed after watching the massacre of their kin and being ravaged by the males of the invading tribes.

Khour's bristly black hair stood up on the middle of his scalp, having been shaved at the sides. It made him look even fiercer. I'd never seen anyone of another race before; our planet had never been visited by anyone from the stars.

I trembled with the overwhelm of all that had happened in such a short amount of time. The acrid smell of smoke stung my nose, the sounds of people writhing in agony in their death throws on the ground assaulted my ears. My friend lay dead—singed by the marauders' magic weapon. That laser was centuries ahead of anything we would have developed on our planet. My people were decimated.

And there stood my mother, tall, proud, and defiant. She didn't cower like the others, she stared that bastard straight in the eye. That must be why his attention narrowed in on her.

"That one," he had said as he pointed with his chin.

My fingers squeeze my thighs so tightly it captures my attention for a moment. A soft growl bubbles from the back of my throat. I don't care if I'm attracting attention from my shipmates, I couldn't control my responses even if I wanted.

I watch in slow motion as my mother is dragged to Khour. She fights, trying to pull away but she's no match for the two large males who have her in their grip. I never realized until just this moment how courageous my mother was to fight them in the face of all their weapons. She stood up to them with nothing but a hayfork. Even after being beaten and ravaged she still fought them.

"Kneel," Khour ordered.

She didn't answer back, just slowly shook her head. He ordered it again, but she continued to shake her head until he grabbed the broadsword offered by the Skylosian chief, strode the five paces to her, and sliced her head off.

My eyes slam closed. I wish I could shut out the vivid picture inside my mind—the way her head fell from her shoulders and landed on the ground.

Prying my eyes open, I force myself back to the present. I can't stay in the past one moment longer. I stare at Willa, hoping it will calm and comfort me, but it doesn't work. She's attuned to me and knows something is terribly wrong. Her concerned gaze undoes me.

I can't speak. The only way I can function is to put my features on lockdown so tightly nothing moves so no emotion can escape. But it doesn't work. I feel the telltale tightening in my chest that signals I'm about to shift. I haven't done so in front of anyone since I came aboard the *Fool's Errand.*

Kill him. WarDog is enraged, growling, snarling, his fangs are dripping with the desire to rip out the throat of the enemy in front of us. I can't stop him. I throw myself to the floor and feel the painful process as, in a matter of *modicums*, my bones change form, muscles rearrange, and my face grows a muzzle. The growl that tears from my throat catches everyone's attention.

I'm sentient in my canine form, just more bestial. I'm a predator with heightened senses and single-minded purpose. Ten *annums* in the arenas where he was forced to fight for his life has changed him from a hunting companion to a killer. WarDog wants him dead and so do I. He killed my mother and members of our tribe, decimated our pack.

He is my enemy. Attack! WarDog growls and snarls then lunges at one of the screens and bites it until I hear a satisfying crunch although his mouth is pierced with pain.

Zar and Shadow jump from their seats, grab him by his mane, and yank him back from the broken screen. He growls loudly, saliva and blood dripping from the cuts in his mouth. The males are strong, but he continues to lunge, trying to break free of their grip. WarDog is out of control.

WarDog stop, I command him but I can't force him to let me shift back.

Willa rushes to him and in spite of the males trying to keep her away, she pushes in and wraps her arms around his neck, whispering calmly into his ear. WarDog resists for a moment, then responds to her gentle touch and voice. I shift, shuddering in her arms.

"Does he do this often Willa?" Zar asks. I'm shocked at how calm he sounds after what just happened. This is one of the many traits that has earned him the title of captain.

"I wasn't aware of any shifts since we came aboard."

The room is silent. Everyone is looking at me. I swipe my mouth with my palm and see blood. When I glance at the vidscreen I see the bite mark.

"Care to tell us what's going on?" Beast asks.

I pull a small shard of glass from my tongue. I'm mortified at my loss of control and that WarDog damaged the vidscreen, but I owe them an answer, "I know that male. I have reason to hate him. He's responsible for the destruction of my home, the deaths of my tribe, my capture, and the ten *annums* of fighting, locked in my canine form," my voice is the same timbre as the growl still resonating from WarDog that I'm barely able to restrain.

"I guess we know what your vote will be," Zar says. "Let's reconvene in two *hoaras*. Enjoy Maddie's feast."

Willa's wide eyes and open mouth indicate her shock at my behavior. My gaze darts from hers and I see similar looks on the faces of the females in the room. The males are all standing with a protective arm around the females with looks of concern mixed with understanding. A wave of guilt washes over me. I terrified the females, terrified Willa. I need to gather control.

"Give me some time in my room," I say as I hurry past her, not wanting to get too close for fear of scaring her even more. Everyone clears a path for me to leave. Filled with shame, I put my head down and rush from the room.

As soon as I'm inside my cabin, I rest my back against the cool metal and force myself to breathe.

Kill him, WarDog insists.

Calm! Is my response.

Placing my palms against the hard surface of the door I return to the present because some of my thoughts are still lodged in the past—in the burning village on Skylose.

I look around the room which holds no personal belongings because I have none. I inventory every stick of furniture and metal rivet on the walls.

I occupy my brain by counting rivets. It soothes me. I allow the past to fade back into my memory. When that doesn't work, I try to shove it back. The picture of my mother's beheading fades to gray, then becomes smaller, then finally disappears. I believe I was happier when I had no recollection of my early life.

As I regain some semblance of peace, my canine stops his furious pacing in my head.

Kill our enemy, tear out his throat, protect Willa. He spears me with his angry stare.

He's practically frothing at the mouth, pushing hard to be released to hunt and kill. He spent too many years in the fighting pits—I can't let him control me. Now he's embarrassed me in front of the males I'm coming to regard as friends. He scared Willa and the other females.

What if I shift and can't change back? I stand over him in my mind, asserting my authority and commanding his obedience. I force him to submit and push him into a corner of my mind until he sits, his head hanging and his eyes cast down.

I hold onto the only thing besides Willa that can give me comfort. Revenge. Zar just gifted me many things. He told me the name of my enemy and gave me the means to vanquish him. I will not rest until that male is dead.

Willa

Bayne's been gone for at least an hour. I gave him space, but now I wonder if he could use the company of a friend, or at least some food.

I juggle a tray heaped with food as I knock on his door. When he doesn't answer, I call, "Bayne! I thought you might be hungry. I'll just leave this plate on the floor out here. Are you okay?"

After waiting a moment, I set the tray down and move to leave. Relief floods me as I hear the pneumatic snick of the opening door.

When I see the expression on his face, my hand flies to my throat in automatic self-protection. His eyes are slit, his nostrils are flaring, but the scariest thing I see are his bared teeth. Is he going to shift again? I shouldn't worry. One thing I know is that no matter what happens, he won't hurt me in his WarDog form.

"Thanks," his tone is a low growl.

"W-want company?"

If I didn't know he was alive I might think he's a statue, that's how still he is as he considers my offer. I hadn't realized it would be such a hard question.

"Yes," he says as he nods tightly. The expression on his face softens and he finally looks me in the eye as if he's seeing me for the first time since the door opened.

After taking the tray from me, he motions me to enter.

"You okay?" I don't want to be intrusive, and doubt he wants to talk, but as of a few hours ago our status was 'in a relationship', so I should at least ask.

He sags onto a chair at the small table in the corner and gestures for me to take the other seat.

"Until recently, I hadn't remembered much about my time before permanently shifting into canine form. Bits and pieces have been sifting in. Seeing Daneur Khour's face filled in many of the blanks. How much do you want to know?"

I grab his hand from his lap and squeeze, making sure I have eye contact. Dear Lord, he looks haunted. Whatever is hiding behind his gorgeous golden gaze must be tragic. The answer to his question is easy. "As much as you feel comfortable telling me, Bayne. Now, or later, or never is okay. Just know one thing. I'm here for you."

He lifts my palm in his and presses it against his cheek, then to his lips for a soft kiss. "Such a good female. I doubt I deserve you.

"Raiders came to my village when I was not yet twenty *annums* old. They set it on fire, molested the females, killed most of the inhabitants. My mother was one of those females. Then they rounded up the males they could repurpose. I was one of those, my function was to fight and make money for my owners. The invaders were led by an offworlder with purple skin. Daneur Khour."

"It all just flooded back?"

He nods.

"Want a hug?"

His answer is to scoot his chair back and open his arms. I sit on his lap and snug my hip against his belly, pressing my cheek against his chest. He's naked since his shift. I hadn't noticed until just now.

There's not much a person can say to a revelation like that. I won't even try. What I can do, though, is provide the comfort of my embrace. He dips his head and lays it on the pillow of my breasts.

As passionate as our lovemaking was last night and this morning, what we're doing right now is far from it. It's interesting that I feel more like a mate now than I did when we were writhing naked in the sheets.

Chapter Eight

Bayne

We're in the *ludus*. Some of us are on the floor, some on weight benches that have been pulled into a circle.

We voted several *hoaras* ago, with a resounding number in favor of attacking our enemy. I assumed the females would all vote no. From talking with many of them over the last *lunar*, I've noticed most of them have gentle souls. By their votes, they've proven their fierce loyalty. They want to protect everyone on these two ships to the best of their ability.

We didn't want to hold this tactical meeting in the dining room. That's where we held a party only last night. It's where we laugh and joke and relax.

No, the place for planning war is in the *ludus*. Though the females call it a gymnasium, it's where we practice our fighting. It's fitting to be here.

Although the females are here with us, it's an unwritten agreement that the males will fight and the females will cheer us on. I'm hungry for revenge, but above all, I want to keep my Willa safe. WarDog is still subdued deep in the recess of my mind, but I feel his agreement. He whines dejectedly, trying to regain my good graces, but I ignore him.

Erro was one of the males who came aboard when Beast killed his former owner and freed the males of his *ludus* on planet Trent. His cabin is on Beast's ship, the *Devil's Playground*. He tells us that he and his brother were both stolen from his homeworld. He was sent to be trained as a gladiator, his brother went to work directly for Khour.

"Since I was freed from Plenum's *ludus*, I've spent every spare moment tracking down my brother, Turk," Erro explains. "I found him about a *lunar* ago and we've engaged in encrypted communications. I discovered where Khour is, and I know some of his habits. It was only yesterday when I brought this information to Beast that we decided to call this meeting.

"Khour has a sprawling compound on planet Fairea. Although the planet is a tourist haven known for what the females call a year-round Renaissance Fair, it has other attractions like relaxed law enforcement and enough traffic coming and going that smuggling is easy.

"Khour's residence is in a huge wooded area far enough away from the tourism to have privacy, but close enough to the action to oversee his gun, drug, and slave-running empire.

"Turk reports that ever since one of the pirates threw acid on Khour's face he rarely leaves his home base. He has a parade of doctors and charlatans coming to the planet. They all promise hope in the way of repairing his face, but Turk says if anything, his face is more ruined than it was before the medics began making pilgrimages there.

"Khour has taken up hunting. Turk jokes that it's the only way he takes out his aggression that doesn't involve harming sentient beings. He's a *motherdracker* of the highest order."

"Or lowest," Stryker quips.

"Yes. Lowest. I was thinking there would be fewer guards on his hunting trips than at any other time of his week. It would be the safest time for us to take him out. That way we wouldn't have to attack his stronghold. I'm told the compound is like a fortress."

Satellite and drone footage appear on the large vidscreen. They show the compound from the air. It's impressive and will be difficult to breach. Turk is right.

A picture of Khour cycles through the vids we're watching and I can't control my growl. Willa's small hand slips around my waist and she tucks her hip closer to mine. Although her presence calms me, WarDog is close to my surface, snarling. Still angry and not wanting a replay of his behavior in the dining room, I force him back to the corner. The lingering taste of blood in my mouth doesn't trouble me, in fact, it spurs me on.

"The forest is thick with trees and brambles. I propose one male go alone for recon. A single male camping alone wouldn't look threatening if Khour's males happen upon him. It could look innocent.

"There would be danger. I think the fewer weapons the volunteer brings the less guilty he will look if he's apprehended and interrogated. No lasers. It might take several days, but the volunteer can gather enough information so our attack can be a surgical strike."

Erro volunteers, as do many of the others.

"I'll go," I say loudly as I stand. "These pictures look a lot like my home planet of Skylose. I lived a simple life there in the forest. This mission was made for me."

"I know you want revenge, Bayne. But we *all* want resolution," Zar says levelly.

"I could hunt in the woods as my cover story. I'm skilled with a bow and arrow and could kill game and keep myself fed until I see him in the woods. I'll comm the ships when I see him. I don't even need to perform the kill, although I'd love to. I'll give you his coordinates so we're guaranteed a hit. I can protect myself without a laser better than anyone onboard—I can shift to my battle form."

I look at the pictures scrolling across the vid screens. The geography is so familiar it could be Skylose.

"I think this is a good plan," Zar says. "It might take days, but we have nothing else more pressing. We can stay in orbit, keep in encrypted communication, and wait until we have the perfect opportunity.

"I'll give this mission two weeks. If Khour doesn't go hunting within that time, we'll have to run with our second plan and attack his stronghold. The hunting ruse will be the best way to avoid loss of life. Does anyone have another idea? Any objections?"

My heart is pounding. I feel proud and excited. I will kill the male who ruined my life, enslaved me for a decade, and destroyed my village. I will make him pay for murdering my mother. I'll exact revenge just as my uncle urged when his wise words kept me alive on that fateful day.

"I'm going with him," Willa stands as she says this. Her shoulders thrust back and her chin tips forward as if she dares anyone to argue with her.

"No," I state it as a simple fact.

"In the dining room, you just showed us that your emotions are involved. Everyone on board this ship has a stake in this mission going smoothly. You're the male for the job, you're correct in that. But I'm the female who is going to support the cover story that we're just hunting. *And* I'll help you keep a calm head."

"It's not safe. You're not equipped."

"I'm from south Texas," she says as if that explains everything. When I continue to shake my head, she explains, "I know how to shoot a gun whether it be rifle or pistol. I can ride a horse with no hands, hunt and skin my own food, and camp in the woods for weeks at a time thanks to my daddy and my daddy's daddy who started taking me on hunting trips when I was seven. Don't tell a Texas girl what she can and cannot do."

She folds her arms across her chest, spears me with a blistering look, and lifts her chin as if she's daring me to argue.

Although I wonder if this might make her change what she calls our relationship status, I repeat, "No. It's not safe. This is a mission for a male."

Every female in the room makes a noise. Some just say, "Ohh," some hiss, and others say, "He did not just say that!" or "You're not going to let him get away with that, are you?"

What did I say wrong? I only want to protect my female.

"You're too emotionally involved, Bayne. I calm WarDog. I did it at lunch and I'll do it on Fairea if needed. I can take care of myself."

We argue for a few more *minimas*, with every soul on board watching. When I saw both Captain Zar's and Captain Beast's mates fold their arms across their chests with looks that had both Captains grimacing, I knew I was fighting a lost cause.

Willa puts her hands on her hips and gives me the same look, her eyes slitted. Even WarDog chimes in, whining. I ignore him.

Maybe Willa's right. As much as I would prefer to have her safe on the ship while I do the mission, I also come to the abrupt realization I don't want to be separated from her ever again.

"I don't like it, Willa, but I can't fight you and everyone else on board. At the first sign of trouble, though, you have to go back to the ship."

"I'm glad you still have two cabins," Petra says after Zar approves my participation in the mission only if Willa accompanies me. "I have a feeling someone's gonna be sleeping in the doghouse tonight." She snickers as her eyes avoid mine. "No offense. It's an Earth saying."

Willa

The last few days have been an education in anxiety—controlled and otherwise. If I had just sat around worrying, I would have nibbled my nails to the quick. Luckily, I've been keeping myself busy.

Dax and Bayne helped me make a bow and arrows. I even have a cool leather quiver. I've been practicing archery in the *ludus*. Although I don't think I could kill any wild game, I will look proficient enough to corroborate our cover story.

We've already docked on Fairea. Bayne and I look like we belong together as we wait for the ramp to lower. We're both wearing tan leather pants and tunics. Dax helped us make soft moccasins, too. I even know what type of game we'll supposedly be hunting, I looked it up on the Database to make sure I could stay completely in character. They're like deer with shockingly ugly heads and four eyes. According to the Database there are no large predators in this part of the planet.

We're parked in one of the offworlder parking lots near the fairgrounds. Most of the people from the *Fool's Errand* visited here a while back and their descriptions were spot-on. It's a giant Renaissance Festival—alien style.

I saw a cornucopia of aliens on Aeon II when I watched the canine shifter match, but it feels different here. At the gladiatorial games, the bloodlust in the air was so thick you could almost taste it. Here at the fair, people are more light-hearted. They're here for a good time that doesn't involve bloodsport.

The reedy sound of a flute drifts to me from my right and primitive drum beats assault my ears from the left. The smell of spitted meat wafts to my nose; I'm sure WarDog must love that.

People are wearing the garb of their ancestors, just as we do at Ren-Fests on Earth. I see everything from loincloths to velvet dresses with as much variation as can be imagined.

We don't enter the fairgrounds, though, we skirt that and head to the hover lot. Shadow will drive us to the forest about an hour away.

After stopping at an outfitter store to stock up on camping necessities, we take off to the west.

Shadow is a large male, wearing his black leather kilt and sash. On the ship, most of the males wear loincloths or nothing at all, but this is like their uniform when we're on land. It makes them look deadly and official, which is the exact impression Shadow is going for.

His left arm looks like it was severed in battle and he wears a high-tech prosthetic. He also has a prosthetic eye. He was a gladiator for a long time, but rumor has it that before his parents sold him into the arena, he was high-born.

I'm not exactly sure what the story is, but rumor also has it that Daneur Khour was part of his fall from grace and descent into slavery.

Shadow's smart and savvy and loves his mate like she hung the moon—or moons depending upon which planet we're on. After he mated Petra, he decided not to fight in the arena anymore, but sometimes I wonder if he misses it.

"Let's go over it again," Shadow says as he competently hovers along the periphery of the vast fairgrounds.

We've drilled this a dozen times in the last few days so I launch without more prompting. "We're Bayne and Willa, no last name. I'm Morganian, he's of unknown parentage and grew up in an orphanage on Aeon II. If asked about specifics, he'll say they didn't allow him out of the building. I investigated the Intergalactic Database enough to be able to answer basic questions about Morgana."

"We're on our sweetmoon," Bayne continues.

"Honeymoon," I gently correct.

"We're on our honeymoon and thought it would be romantic to live on the land, so we could rely on each other. We own a farm on Nativus."

The three of us are sitting abreast in the front of the hover, our supplies are in the back.

Before I can continue with my canned speech, Bayne looks me in the eye, and says, "Willa, please go back to the ship," his tone is a combination of an order and a plea. "This is too dangerous."

Smart male. Over the last few days, I at least broke him of the habit of telling me it was too dangerous for a *female*.

We've had this argument over several breakfasts, lunches, and dinners as well as upon rising in the morning and before bedtime. It's been between us like a living thing.

"I calm you, Bayne, and I think you might need me at your side to keep from shifting. Even Captain Zar agreed the honeymoon gave us a great cover story, and I've gotten pretty good with the bow and arrow."

"You're barely proficient at it, Willa. And you're so small. And soft. And I don't want you hurt."

How can I not be falling for this guy? Look at his face, his golden eyes swirling with passion. He may sound controlling, but it's obvious he just wants to protect me. What female wouldn't want that?

"It's decided," I say as I place a soft hand on his thigh. "I'll be here with you. It's just a recon mission."

I think he has an ulterior motive. I believe he's hoping to not just find Daneur Khour, but to kill him.

"Shadow, promise me someone will be at the comms station every moment. If we need help—"

"You don't need to ask, brother," Shadow interrupts him. "We have your back. The captains want the ships cleaned down to the seams in the metal while we're waiting for your call. Trust me, we'll be doing nothing more important than tuning into the comm frequency, ready to drop everything to help you. Gladiators will be armed and stationed at the transporter, ready to beam down at a moment's notice."

We've left the hubbub of the fair, and are hovering toward an expansive forest. Farther west I see what looks like a small city.

"Khour's compound," Shadow informs us.

"Whoa!"

First of all, I didn't imagine it would be . . . beautiful. Even though we saw it on vid, I didn't realize how large it really is. There is one huge main building which Shadow says is Khour's mansion, and dozens of smaller outbuildings. The entire complex is made of rock cut by the finest artisans and pieced together in a kind of checkerboard of chestnut and gold stone.

It looks as if much of the compound is old, maybe many centuries. The mansion seems to have been added recently. It was designed to fit in with the rest, though, retaining the same checkerboard look with stones cut and pieced together to look as if they're from the same slab of rock.

Is that an old covered well in the middle of all the structures? It almost reminds me of a feudal lord's compound—or a fairytale. Too bad such an evil bastard lives here. I'm sure Khour loves being lord of his castle.

"I guess burning it down is out of the question," Bayne says glumly.

"No. Stone doesn't burn," Shadow agrees, "but it's not impervious to lasers." He banks hard to the right and lowers us so we're skimming so close to the treetops my hands grab my thighs in terror.

"Tell me when you see a campsite you like. We'll find you something easily defensible."

"There," Bayne points off to the right. The trees are thicker there, and there's an outcropping of rock maybe twenty feet high that we can shelter against.

Shadow can't set the hover down close to the spot because the forest is so dense, but an hour later we've carried our supplies to our campsite, he's helped us set up a space-age tent, and he bids us goodbye.

"We're standing by, you two. All we need to know is when he's in this forest, his coordinates, and an estimate on how many males he has with him. We'll do the rest, and you two will remain safe." He swings through the hover doorway, then leans out to tip his head and smile as he tells us, "You might as well have some fun."

After he leaves, I take the opportunity to investigate our campsite. It's quiet here, and although it doesn't remind me of where I used to hunt in Texas, it does remind me of how much I love to revel in nature.

The temperature feels like the high eighties, but here in the shade, it's comfortable. The round-leaved trees form a canopy overhead, and I hear birds calling to each other all over the forest.

When I used to hunt with my dad or granddad, the sounds of nature and the wind on my face soothed me. When I glance at Bayne, the tightness of his features tells a different story. He's not having calm, fond memories. Is he back in his village, watching invaders burn it to the ground?

"I wish you weren't here, Willa. I wish it with all my heart," he looks at me, eyebrows pulled down tightly in concern. "We're in a relationship. In my world, that means it's my responsibility to keep you safe. I've met this male, he was evil and heartless years ago, and he's only grown more powerful since then. I don't want you on the same planet as him, much less so close to his property."

My heart swells with affection as my eyes grow misty. We only crossed the line from 'it's complicated' to 'in a relationship' three days ago, but I wonder if I'm falling in love with him. 'It's complicated' includes a humungous four-legged dog with razor-sharp teeth, but now that I've met the caring male underneath the fur, it hardly seems worth factoring into the equation.

"It makes me feel so cared for that you want to protect me, Bayne. If the situation changes, I'll comm the ship and have them beam me up. Until then, you're stuck with me." I waggle my eyebrows at him, suddenly in a hurry to unpack our bedroll. From the pictures at the outfitter shop that showed a thick air mattress the size of a queen bed, this is about as close to glamping as I'll ever get.

The tent is amazing. Actually calling it a tent is like calling the Grand Canyon a ditch. The tent is a see-through sphere made of thin plastic. With the touch of a button, it somehow fills with air, inflates, and voila, we've got shelter. Not just shelter, but we can see the sun rise and set. It's going to be romantic.

We unpack the six-inch cube which inflates with a press of a button to a ten-inch thick mattress, organize our food and cooking supplies, and neaten our little 'sweetmoon' suite. Is he adorable or what?

It's mid-afternoon, we have plenty of time until supper . . . and bed. I wonder when I'll tell him Dr. Drayke informed me the contraceptive implant he gave me is now effective.

"Let's explore," he says. His muscles are loose for the first time in days. After we shrug our quivers and bows over our shoulders, he grabs my hand, and we strike off.

Bayne

The trees in the forest have little round leaves that flutter in the warm breeze. The area we enter is so dense, not much sunlight penetrates the canopy above.

I sniff the air to find the scent of predators, but only smell small birds and little woodland mammals. My ears prick as I listen for danger, but there's nothing nearby to fear.

It feels like an eternity since I've felt my canine run in a place like this, so long since I've been in my shifted form for anything other than fighting. Both WarDog and I are anxious to feel the dirt under his paws again.

Even though I'm still upset with WarDog, I know I may need him to fight or protect Willa. I call him forward and call a truce. His head raises expectantly and his tail unfurls from between his legs. When I encourage him to come out for a run, his tail thumps happily.

"Willa, stay here. Please don't stray. I won't be gone long, I just need to . . ." I shrug.

"Okay. Have fun."

I didn't even have to tell her what I wanted to do, she knew. She's so accepting of who I am. I remove my weapons, pull my clothes off and set them in a neat pile, then walk a few steps away.

Mate, WarDog says happily as we glance back at her.

The shift is easy and painless, just as it used to be back on Skylose when we functioned as a team.

WarDog is cautious at first, wanting to make sure he stays in my good graces. But after a moment, neither of us can hold back. The world of smells opens and his canine nose sniffs wildly at every blade of grass, every pile of leaves, and every flower.

The feeling of dirt and loam squeezing beneath the pads of his feet reminds us of fun days as a youngling when we ran for *hoaras* until we were lost, then he scented our way home.

Run, WarDog says in ecstasy.

Free, I say, reveling in being able to feel the wind ruffle his fur.

Willa doesn't leave our minds for long. After our quick romp, our duty to protect overrides our joy in exploring our surroundings. We circle back and see her still standing, her back against a tree as a physical sign of her commitment not to move, then we allow ourselves the joy of the chase.

WarDog's muscles feel loose as he trots and then runs in one direction and then another. The delight of pulling out all the stops, of pushing his body to its limits is so freeing. His paws pound the soft ground, his chest expands with huge inhalations, his breath escapes in hot gusts.

How did I live for a decade without this? We both feel fully alive here in the woods, his strides covering the forest floor almost effortlessly.

When we circle back to Willa for the third time, WarDog does more than give her a quick glance. He drinks her in with such affection. I've been so mad at him for getting out of control and embarrassing me in front of everyone on board not one but two ships, but I can't deny we're together for a reason.

We make a good team. And we'll always be linked by our love for that female. Maybe part of the reason I resent him is that he had her to himself for so long when I was locked, virtually unconscious, inside.

Had enough for now? I ask him, wanting to shift back into two-legged form so I can kiss her smiling lips.

More later? He's tired, his tongue is lolling out of his mouth.

Yes. I promise.

He sits at her feet. Willa gives his ruff a vigorous rubdown, digging her fingers deep into the fur, reaching skin. His tail wags so hard dirt and leaves are flying. His eyes close in canine bliss. She laughs and gives him a kiss on the nose.

I missed her so much, he says to me on a heartfelt sigh. WarDog gives her one last adoring look, and I come out.

Willa

Bayne is standing a few feet away, unable to hide his happy, relaxed smile. He steps into his pants and slings his bow and quiver over his shoulder. When he returns to my side, the feeling of Déjà vu is so strong the hair on the back of my neck stands on end.

The huntsman!

The dream has faded enough that I don't think I'll ever clearly remember the huntsman's features, but everything else is exactly as it was a month ago in my dream. From the pelt on his shoulders, which is his real ruff of hair, to the bow and arrows. He's my huntsman.

Sometimes the universe conspires against you. I felt that way when I woke aboard the Urlut slave ship on my way to God knows where. I felt it again when I was roughly tossed into a cell with two huge alien gladiators and a dog whose shoulders were taller than my waist. And again when it was clear the slave ship was being fired upon and I thought my death was imminent.

Sometimes, though, I guess the universe conspires *with* you. That dream was a gift, signaling me that something wonderful was coming my way.

I debate for a moment, wondering if Bayne will judge me or decide I'm crazy, but finally I blurt, "I dreamed this, Bayne. I dreamed every detail of this. The sun dappling through the leaves, the thick trees, even the rich smell of the loam and decomposing leaves.

"Mostly, though I dreamed of you."

His eyes flash to mine, alight with an unspoken question, I'm certain he sees the sincerity written there.

Although we've devoured each others' bodies a dozen times in the last few days, I feel shy, but not too shy to share, "That morning, before we left the ship for Aeon II, when I . . ." I scold myself not to give up now, "pleasured myself. It was after the dream where I met you for the first time. I called you the huntsman in my mind."

He stalks to me, his footsteps silent on the carpet of damp leaves. He places his palm at the nape of my neck and pulls me to him—almost rough, but not harsh. He's full of passion. "What did this huntsman do?" his voice is gruff, almost a growl.

"He didn't speak at all. We came together without a word. Our bodies spoke to each other. It was magnificent."

With his hand on my neck, he walks me backward until the quiver on my back hits a tree. After shrugging it off, I feel the rough, cool bark through my leather tunic.

"He took you? Here in the woods?" his tone is breathy, his expression earnest, as if he wants to know every detail in order to get it right.

I nod.

"Without a word?"

I nod again.

He slants his mouth and takes my lips so hard my head knocks gently against the tree. His grip on my neck is tight, slightly uncomfortable, a silent reminder that he's in complete control. Just this kiss and his rigid hold on me, and I feel my arousal spiraling higher.

He bends his knees so when he grinds his hips against me the hard ridge of his cock presses right where I need it most.

Much of the time he keeps his teeth hidden behind his perfect lips, but not now. They're on full display. My channel clenches in desire as I recall the faint sting the sharp tips of his fangs make as they scrape along my delicate flesh when he's in the height of passion.

Maybe it's the primitive setting, but he's discarded the trappings of civilization we usually cling to onboard the *Fool*. He *is* my huntsman!

His hips grind rhythmically, his fangs graze me, and he's making low growling noises in the back of his throat. If he had done this the first time we had sex, I would have freaked out. Now, just a few days later, it makes me want him so badly I sink my fingers into the pelt at his shoulders, pulling him to me so tightly he won't be able to walk away.

I jump up and straddle him so he doesn't have to bend to press himself against me. This allows him to thrust *and* grind, adding so much to both our pleasure I find myself mimicking his eager noises from the back of my throat.

His tongue penetrates me in the same rhythm as his hips and I wonder how many more thrusts it will take, even through the layers of our clothes, to bring my release.

His snarl is louder now, a different timbre; it's distinctive. He snakes his hands under my tunic, then slides them up my midriff until he cups the full weight of my breasts in his palms. Although we haven't been lovers long, he's already learned how anticipation makes me want him all the more. His thumbs make hot figure-eights on my ribs, promising so much pleasure when he decides to drag them higher.

We both realize at the same moment that something isn't right. I don't know if we heard a noise, or just felt a shift. He slides me down so my feet are on the soft carpet of decomposing leaves and twirls to look behind him.

Not twenty feet away is the ugliest thing I've ever seen. My first thought is that it's a combination of a tarantula and a scorpion. It's four-feet tall and disgustingly shaggy with the gross hairy ick-factor of a huge spider combined with the pincers and deadly tail of a scorpion.

Its deadly front pincers are strong and large enough to snap my neck. Its high, flat tail is cocked threateningly. Its circular black mouth opens side-to-side instead of up and down.

I can't control a shiver of revulsion while at the same moment fear slices through me. The hideous thing clicks its pincers and then scuttles straight toward us on hard black insectoid feet, all six of them.

Bayne stands staunchly between the thing and me, using his back to press me against the tree trunk. He's already pulled his bow off his shoulder, nocked an arrow, and let it fly. It pierces the animal through its shoulder. There was no way to aim for its heart because it's standing with its chest parallel to the ground.

I fumble with my bow and am still scrambling to pluck an arrow from my quiver when the thing hisses, then spits. Bayne isn't deterred, he just lets another arrow fly, this time piercing the thing directly through one of its two beady eyes. It lets loose a high piercing whine, takes two steps toward us, then falls to its side—dead.

At least I think it's dead, who knows how alien tarantu-scorps' bodies function? I don't see its chest moving, but on other planets can things reanimate?

Bayne unsheathes the knife on his belt and strides toward the thing. With the six-inch knife in one hand, he pulls his arrows out with the other. The wet-squishy sound the arrow makes when he removes it from the animal's eye makes me swallow hard. I shake my head as if to get the image and sound out of my mind. It's one of those things you know with certainty you'll remember in detail many years into the future.

Bayne pierces me with a knowing stare and doesn't miss the telltale signs of my discomfort. "Are you okay, Willa?" He stands, then seems torn between approaching to give me comfort and wiping the blood and guts off the arrows.

"You don't need to come near me with those," I tell him, wondering where the other Willa is. The Willa who learned how to field dress a deer before her tenth birthday.

He lets them fall from his hand and stalks toward me. "You're not okay," he announces. "You're shaking."

I feel all of five years old, wanting to deny the obvious and tell him I'm not shaking because as sure as I'm standing here, if I admit it he's going to urge me to go back to the ship. So I just stand here paralyzed, my gaze flicking between my handsome huntsman and the huge dead arthropod whose little hairy mouthparts are still quivering.

He folds me in his arms and turns me so his back is against the tree. This accomplishes three things. He can watch over my shoulder to protect me, I'm facing away from the disgusting scene of carnage, and his warmth and compassion can seep into me.

"It's okay, my Willa," he croons, his capable hands sifting through my hair. "I want you to go back to the ship. It's not safe for you here."

I knew that was coming. Truth be told, my feelings would have been hurt if he hadn't offered. I'll be honest with myself, I volunteered—no I didn't exactly volunteer, I demanded—to come more because I didn't want to be separated from my huntsman and less to protect and soothe him.

I stroke up and down along either side of the quiver still on his back. He feels good, solid, reassuring under my fingertips.

"I want to stay with you." I did an adequate job of sounding assertive rather than whiney.

"We've fought this battle before, so I won't argue. I'll just tell you one more time that I'd feel much better with you back on the *Fool's Errand.* Because I . . ." He interrupts his own sentence to kiss me. Not a hard, passionate kiss like before we were interrupted, but a soft, heartfelt one.

Was he about to tell me he loves me? By the look in those gorgeous, golden swirling eyes, I think maybe he was.

His tongue has breached my mouth and is stroking mine in long licks, reminding me there's a dog inside him. A strong warrior capable of protecting me.

It's dimmer in the forest than it had been, at least one of Fairea's three suns must be about to set.

Bayne must have noticed it, too, because he says, "We should get back to camp before it gets dark."

As we walk, I keep my hand on my bow, ready to go into hunting mode in case one of those ugly scuttling *things* darts out of the growing shadows. I wasn't much help when we were being attacked; I vow not to play the helpless female in the future.

We arrive back at the clear orb made out of what on Earth would be thick see-through plastic. I have no idea what material it is out in space, but it's durable and will allow us to see the stars and wake with the sun.

Perhaps I didn't think it through fully, because it will also allow every predator within a mile to see us, and the idea of making love in a see-through enclosure, especially so soon after the tarantu-scorp attack is not appealing.

"Are you sure this tent was a good choice?" I ask, picturing all the little woodland creatures grabbing seats outside our tent, popping some popcorn, and watching us get it on. I decide right here, right now, that will not be happening tonight.

"No. You were busy asking the shopkeeper about the ingredients in the food packets when Shadow and I were making the purchase. It was the only thing available. We're out in the open this way. I don't like it at all."

"At least we're in agreement on that."

We zip ourselves inside the sphere, I toss a thick comforter on top of the cushy bed. I wonder if maybe I was wrong about the no-nookie decision. All the little creatures could see would be the covers wiggling.

We have two comfy camping chairs, and the food packets heat themselves when you shake them. I have no idea what *larg* with *vertiga* and *rendivar* is, and couldn't really get a feel for it from the picture on the package, but that's what I pick to eat tonight. Bayne prefers meat—any type of meat. So he's having a large serving of *hensis*.

We haven't had a chance to talk a lot these past few days; we were too busy getting ready for this mission. Between sewing our own leather clothes, making shoes, and trying to perfect my skills with a bow and arrow, there wasn't a lot of time for casual conversation.

"Tell me about your home planet," I say around a bite of *larg*. The package should have been labeled, 'Tastes Like Ass'.

The muscles on his face tighten as he looks down for a moment. Shit. Bad question. But then he gives me full eye contact as if he decided to focus on everything about his life before the invaders came.

"It was a simple place. There weren't any machines. It was a village with small houses made of saplings that were positioned in circular rows around one longhouse in the middle. That was where I recall the best times of my life." A small smile lifts the corners of his mouth and his gaze darts to mine. It's so good to see him have warm memories.

Chapter Nine

Bayne

Being trapped in canine form for so long muddled my thoughts. It's a wonder I didn't become feral. One good thing came of it, though, memories of my homeworld got lost in the fog. I've been bombarded with them since my return to two legs, and none of them were good. Now, though, sitting with my female, I'd like to page through them. If my thoughts get drawn to the bad times, Willa will pull me back.

"You might call it primitive, but it felt right to me. We were a warrior people, but it was out of necessity. There were many tribes, all vying for land and resources. We rarely killed each other, though. We vanquished by stealing livestock or driving them out of the fertile valley where we wanted to make our camp."

"Sounds kind of like the Native Americans on Earth. They used to count coup, which meant riding up to an enemy and touching them with a short stick and riding away unscathed. I think it was a show of courage for prestige more than aggression."

"So you understand." He smiles at that and nods. "My father died right after my Spirit Quest ceremony. It's when a boy becomes a male. I had to live on my own in the wilderness for ten days. A boy is sent out naked, with no food, clothes, or weapons, and is left on his own. When I returned, I felt like a full-grown male.

"Not only did I have no one to rely on but myself during those ten days, but I became closer to my canine form. We are born in our humanoid form but are able to shift by the time we reach five or six *lunars*. We worked together on my Spirit Quest more closely than we ever had. It was harsh and difficult and the best time of my life."

In my mind, WarDog is lying with his head on his paws, his ears perked forward, tail wagging slowly, he sighs with contentment as I reminisce.

Yes, the best, he agrees.

Willa nods approvingly and says nothing. It's one of the things I like best about her, she can tolerate the silences. I feel closest when we sit in the quiet together.

"And you, Willa? What of your life before you met me?"

"I guess females don't need to go on Spirit Quests to declare we're adults. We know when we're women—nature makes a big red announcement." She shrugs. "So mom died right around then and it was just me and dad and grandad.

"I liked digging in our huge backyard garden as a child. When mom died I loved growing all sorts of vegetables to go with the meat we hunted and those we had on the farm. I loved climbing trees, hunting, and camping. I was a tomboy. Did that translate?"

I shake my head.

"A girl who likes to do what boys do. I was never into frilly dresses or dances."

Her eyes fly to mine. I guess we're both thinking of the dance the other night.

"You seemed to enjoy the dance on the *Fool*. And I have to say I enjoyed your dress even if you didn't," my voice is deep and rough as my gaze makes a slow slide all the way from her pink lips to her toes.

"Well, yeah. I guess I've grown to like those things, too."

Mate. This conversation caught WarDog's attention. *Mount her, make her ours.* He wants to mate her. He's wanted this since that first day in the cell when her fingers slipped under his ruff and stroked all the best spots as if someone had drawn her a map. She gave him a name like they were best friends. How could either of us not grow to love her?

Love. Is that what this is? I wish my mother was alive. She'd explain my complicated emotions. In our tribe sex was freely shared between mature males and females in humanoid and canine forms. I have never felt like this with any female I've lain with. Sharing with only one partner was reserved for mated couples.

Although actually there's nothing complicated about how I'm feeling. I like this female, I have affection for her. I want to mount her, but it's so much deeper than that. Most of all, I want to protect her.

I push WarDog back. He resists but then gives up and lies down with his head on his front paws.

"I wish you'd go back to the *Fool*," I blurt before I know the words have flown from my mouth. Glancing down, I have the good sense to act contrite, knowing she doesn't like me telling her what to do.

"I know."

"You say you want to protect me and keep me in humanoid form, but *I* protected *you* today. My belly clenches in fear just thinking what that animal might have done to you."

When the picture of that thing spearing her with one of its deadly pincers darts into my brain, I wonder if I could go on without her. The thought slams into me that I already think of Willa as my mate. I'll need to tell her.

Soon, WarDog agrees.

"Can I convince you to return to the ship?" I ask, knowing the answer.

She shakes her head, but does it with a smile. Not just any smile, but the slight tip of her lips that is an invitation for kissing . . . and more.

"I'm a canine. I have a strong need to assert dominance," I warn as I rise to my feet. In my mind, WarDog leaps to his feet, too, his whole body at attention.

Sniffing deeply he urges, *She wants us. Take her, hold her, bite her, make her ours.*

NO, I snarl, our truce forgotten as jealousy overtakes me, *she wants me not you. Back off.* His head drops, his tail slips between his legs and he slinks out of sight.

Oblivious to my inner struggle with my beast, Willa responds, "I'm a female," she says with a toss of her long brown hair, "I have a strong desire to feel dominated." Her smile isn't slight anymore, it's welcoming. "Some of the time," she adds with a shrug of one shoulder.

I practically leap to bridge the distance between us. Pulling her to her feet, I grab her shoulders and slant my lips across hers in a claiming kiss. I'm addicted to her taste. It reminds me of the warm sunshine back home.

"I know we don't want younglings, but as soon as it's safe, I want to take you," I growl into her ear, then assault her mouth as if it's an enemy encampment. I would be taking her by force, except she puts up no resistance as I slide into the warm recesses of her mouth, tasting and tempting in return.

Her fingers lodge in my ruff. She must love the feel. Her fingers always rest there when I'm nearby whether I'm in humanoid or canine form.

"Make love with me, Bayne."

"Yes. When it's safe."

"It *is* safe. The doc said as of today it's working, and it's completely reversible if we want to change things in the future."

I pull back to look at her by the light of the laser lantern. As I inspect her face, I see no deception, just sincerity and urgent need.

My cock, already hard and wanting, twitches in my pants at the idea of taking her fully tonight. I can't mate her, I know. We haven't discussed it. She'd need to understand what she would be getting into and agree to it. But just the thought of sliding into her wet heat makes me more excited than I've ever been.

I loosen the latigo cords holding the top of her tunic together, then gather the hem between my fingers and pull it over her head.

"I want you so much, my Willa," I whisper in her ear. "Tell me you're ready for this."

"I want you too, Bayne."

To add truth to her words, her cool palms slide over my hot flesh to my waist, then rise to burrow into the pelt at my shoulders. I nip down the side of her neck, loving her sharp intake of breath when my fangs graze her skin.

She nips me back. If she was canine, her gentle nip might break my skin. As it is, though, her flat blunt teeth just tell me how much she wants me.

She eagerly pulls my loincloth below my knees, leaving it to me to step out of it because her hands are busy roaming across my ass.

"You're the sexiest male I've ever known," she says as her palms skim my flesh as if she wants to be certain to touch every spot on my body.

I'm planning what I want to do to her with as much care and precision as my tribe would prepare for an enemy invasion. I debate whether to conquer her slow and tender or hard and fast. Should I build her to the peak of pleasure with my mouth first, or let us come together quickly in the way we've been avoiding for days?

"Make love with me, Bayne. I need you," she says, as her hand slides around my hip and grips my hard cock at the root. "We've waited long enough."

WarDog is close, urging me on, flooding me with baser needs I usually keep at bay. I don't shift, but it feels like my fangs elongate, making it easier for me to slide their tips along her tender flesh.

Again, I feel a surge of resentment. He had her to himself for three *lunars.* What we're about to do is for me, not him. I force him back, *Stay there or I will leash you,* I threaten. He cowers, whimpers, and obeys. I get a sudden twinge of guilt for treating him like this after he has had to endure ten *annums* of enslavement, but I quickly tamp it down, force my attention from my interfering canine, and focus on the delectable female before me.

Careful not to prick her skin, I glide my fangs down the column of her neck and across her collar bone. This causes her to lift on her toes with a little shiver.

"Do that again," her whisper is deep and breathy.

I oblige, shaking my head back and forth across the skin-covered bone. The scent of her arousal blooms on the air. I mimic my actions on her other collarbone and hear her suck in air as if the sheer pleasure surprises her.

I trace my fangs lower, over the gentle rise of her breast, then across the pink crest.
This pulls an appreciative hum from the back of her throat.

My hands are nestled just below her waist in the valley just before the swell of her shapely ass. Moving them lower, I cup her ass cheeks and yank her against me, grinding my cock along her seam, my knees bent so they're the right height to provide her pleasure.

She mirrors my actions, her hands on my cheeks, ensuring we stay pressed together as she rides me, coating me with the slick evidence of her desire.

It feels like I've waited an eternity for this, even though it's been a mere handful of days since we acknowledged our feelings for each other. We're both ready, though. WarDog's urges amplify my own desires. If I don't keep control of him I might act rougher than Willa wants.

She pulls away enough that I feel cool night air against my skin where her warm skin had been. Grabbing my hand, she attempts a smile, but she's too deep in the well of passion to pull it off. It's too serious, too needy to look happy. It's sexier than that and intensifies my desire.

Dragging me toward the bed, her brown eyes gaze deeply into mine. Her expression speaks of want and need and desperation, and so much more. I respond, my eyes blazing with my own story of affection for her.

She sits on the edge of the bed and pats the spot next to her. I don't want to join her there, not yet. I want to taste her again. I've wondered if her taste is addictive, but decided it's not the taste, but the feeling of being the one responsible for providing her bliss. I love the sensation of giving her pleasure, the sounds of her moans and heavy breathing.

The canine inside me, a moment ago fully submissive, jumps up and barks, his hackles rising along his spine.

Trouble, he snarls, capturing my attention. I follow the direction of his thoughts and look out through the clear tent.

My blood runs cold as I freeze, my mind flying through every strategy I can use to keep us alive.

"Grab your bow and arrows! Now!" I tell her.

Somewhere in the dim recesses of my mind, I'm proud of our connection. Willa doesn't pause a *modicum*, she follows my orders immediately without question.

"Shit!" she sounds panicked.

As soon as she was alerted to the urgency of the situation by the tone of my voice, she became more aware of our surroundings. It isn't hard to miss the dozen creatures that have surrounded the clear globe we thought ensured our comfort. They're the same as the animal I killed this afternoon. Willa called them tarantu-scorps.

The tent provides protection from the elements, but I could easily slice through it with my fang. Certainly, these creatures, with their deadly pincers could slash it with little effort. I've bent and retrieved my bow and hung my quiver on my back. I don't know why they haven't attacked already. I'm sure it's imminent.

I tear my eyes from the scene outside the globe to glance at Willa. She's standing, bow drawn, her quiver over her shoulder.

"Stand back to back with me, Love. I'm better with a bow than you, but you'll have to help. We're vastly outnumbered. You only have twelve arrows, make them count."

We only have twenty-four arrows between us, and who knows how many creatures are out there. My guess is a dozen, but there could be an army of them hiding farther away in the shadows.

The calm continues for only a moment more, then all of them step forward at once. Do they have a hive mind? That will make them even more deadly adversaries. Several of them use their front pincers to horizontally slash the tent material. The now detached top of the structure blows away in the light breeze getting caught in a nearby tree. In that one moment, we're completely exposed and unprotected.

I feel Willa's warm back against mine and take a moment to pray she can live through this assault. The best thing I can do to help her is to kill the enemy.

No thoughts fly through my head, my hands take charge—they move faster than I can think. They proceed on their own accord, reaching behind me to grab an arrow, nocking it, and letting fly. It penetrates directly where I was aiming—the beady black eye. An otherworldly shriek pierces the air, and the animal staggers, then falls.

"Aim for the eyes if you can, Love," I remind her. Because of the way the creatures are built, it's hard to aim for the heart.

"Right," her voice is tight. She's fully concentrating on her task. Good.

I don't know if the animals have some sense of what their pack is thinking, but a few attack as the rest wait and watch, coming at us in waves. I don't take my eyes off my foe for a heartbeat, but worry about Willa. I pull my thoughts to the task at hand. I'm not protecting my female if I remain unfocused.

I've felled six of them with eight arrows, their hairy corpses litter the bed and floor of the structure. Their comrades keep on coming, stepping over their felled packmates and forging ahead.

Willa and I are well attuned to each other. When I turn, her body naturally follows my motion. When the enemy in front of me has stopped aggressing, I turn us so I can help on her side of the melee.

I'm proud when I see three felled beasts on her side of the clearing. Launching three arrows in swift succession, I kill three more.

"How many left?" I ask when I've turned us in our original directions.

"Four arrows, one beast," she answers, evidently not knowing whether I was asking about arrows or animals.

"Two left on my side," I tell her.

"Shit!" she says after launching an arrow, then, "Gotcha, bastard!"

Both the creatures in front of me attack at once. The ungainly beasts move swiftly when they want to. I shoot my arrows quickly, but after felling one of the two, my next shot misses its mark.

As I pull another arrow from my quiver, I hear the squealing whine of the last beast in the throes of death—Willa killed him with her last arrow.

I hear her panting, feel her torso heaving since our backs are still pressed together. We rotate in a complete circle, both of us wanting to ensure no more of the ugly beasts are creeping up on us in the darkness.

We continue to circle. In the relative calm, we both realize we forgot to call for backup.

She says, "The comms!" as I call into my comm, "Beam us up."

"Wait!" she says a moment later as she pulls a tunic over her head. "Okay," she tells them.

I don't know why I didn't call for help a moment ago. The heat of battle put the idea of rescue by beaming my particles through the air completely out of my mind.

Soon Willa and I are standing on the *Fool's Errand*, panting, bows in hand, backs pressed together.

Willa

My heart is pounding in my chest, my hands, rock steady until a moment ago, are fluttering.

I handled the height of battle like a champ. Now, though, I'm having a complete breakdown. What was I thinking? I forced myself onto that mission. Just because I'm a strong Texas girl and know how to kill a deer with a rifle does not mean I had any business going to a foreign planet with a bow and fucking arrows. Against monsters!

Bayne spun on his heel and is facing me now. He squeezes me in a bear hug, then pulls away to look into my face.

"You're not okay?" he asks, concern written all over his beautiful face.

"You saved my life. I'm an idiot."

He presses my face to his chest and strokes my hair. "Not an idiot," he says. I feel his chest rumble as I hear the warm words. "Stubborn."

I'm trembling and crying. I try to convince myself it's the aftermath of the fight, the adrenaline. I don't want to admit it's from sheer terror, albeit delayed.

Captain Zar crashes through the transporter room doorway.

"Are you both alright?" his growly voice is deeper than usual.

"Unharmed," Bayne informs him, then bends to peer into my face. "You *are* unharmed, right?"

"Yes." I nod. "Just about to come unglued, that's all."

"I want a full report. I know you want some time to gather yourselves, but I need to know what happened."

I understand. He has no idea if we were attacked by mutant creatures straight out of a 1950s B movie or Daneur Khour himself.

He leads the way to the bridge and we follow. Most of our little family not-so-subtly line the halls to see what's going on. Several of the women call, "I hope everything's all right, Willa." A few offer for me to come see them if I need anything. There's nothing wrong with me that a long shower and a moment in Bayne's arms won't cure.

Once on the bridge, we give report, and by 'we' I mean Bayne. He's sitting in the first mate's seat, with me on his lap, his arms warmly tucking me against him.

"Take a few *hoaras* to decompress," Zar instructs. "We'll meet in the *ludus* after dinner to plan our next strategy. I'm proud of you," he says warmly, "both of you."

While we were talking, Callista on comms pulled up satellite footage of the carnage at our campsite. It's barely visible through the thick canopy of trees and fading light. She displays it on every other window on the bullet-shaped bridge. The windows double as screens. I just let my eyelids flicker closed, not wanting to see the taratu-scorps for one more moment, but when I get up to leave, I can't help but see the tableau on Fairea.

The creatures are even more gross and scary now. Seeing their disgusting dead bodies, legs akimbo, the area littered with blood, makes me shiver in revulsion.

"As I said," Zar repeats, "you did well. I apologize. I would have never let you go so unprepared had I known, but there was no description of these creatures in the planet's database. Perhaps Khour has brought them from another planet to dissuade people from entering the forest that surrounds his compound. Or perhaps he gets perverted pleasure in hunting them himself. I should have never let you go. In the future, no one goes back to that planet without lasers."

Zar bows his head and thumps his chest at Bayne. It's an honor one gladiator gives another—a sign of the utmost respect. It makes me feel good for Bayne. For so long he was in canine form, fighting in the arena. Now he's getting recognition for what he did. He deserves it.

Zar turns to me and performs the same actions in my direction, his gaze never leaving mine. Did he just give me the gladiator salute? Me? I'm practically dissolving into a puddle of fear.

"You did well, Willa. You killed many of the creatures. You have the spirit of a warrior."

"Th-thanks." It may not be true, but just hearing that I have the spirit of a warrior makes me feel like one.

Perhaps Zar read my thoughts, because he adds, "Courage isn't the absence of fear. It's the ability to do what needs to be done despite your fears."

Wow! No wonder Zar was voted captain, he has wisdom and compassion.

Bayne places his warm palm on the small of my back and escorts me out of the room and back to my cabin. The moment the door closes behind us, he turns me in his arms and hugs me tight.

"I failed you, Willa. I shouldn't have let you come with me."

"Please, Bayne. Stop blaming yourself. You tried everything you could short of forbidding me to go, which would have hurt our relationship more than what happened on Fairea just now. Let it go. I feel like I have tarantu-scorp blood all over me and all I want is a shower."

"You do."

"What?"

"You do have blood on you. It's black, so I know it isn't yours."

"Ack! Out of my way!" Although I'm ready to barge right through him to get to the bathroom, he sidesteps just in time. If circumstances were different, I'd love for him to join me. We've shared a shower several times. It's great foreplay. Now I just want the black bug blood off me. Immediately!

I turn on the water and step in before it's warm. Keeping my eyes closed, I let the water pour over me until I assume all the blood has washed down the drain, then I open my eyes and wash. And scrub. And wash some more. At times the pictures of what just happened flash into my mind. Other times I hear the bugs' high screams of pain as if they were in the shower with me.

Eventually, I wrap what happened into a little box inside my mind and stow it away in the back attic where I keep the really painful memories of my mom during the last part of her illness, and the regret that I'll never see my dad again. Bye-bye tarantu-scorps. I relegate that to the back of my mind too.

Taking a deep breath, I allow my thoughts to move to more pleasant things. Bayne's outside this door. He had some blood on him, too.

"Water's at a premium on a ship, babe," I call to him. "I think we should conserve and wash together, don't you?"

He opens the door immediately, he was obviously waiting for my invitation. "Close brushes with death tend to do strange things to people," he says. "I saw it all the time on Skylose."

He joins me in the shower, his eyes blazing in passion.

"What type of strange things?" I ask, a sexy smile slashed across my face.

"It's so hard to explain."

I watch as the warm water pours down on him and his eyes brighten as he looks at me.

"Let me show you instead."

His head dips toward me, those plump sexy lips unerringly finding mine. "I worried about you," he husks into my ear to be heard over the running water.

"It was scary," I admit.

"I have you now. You're here in my arms. This is how it should be."

His golden gaze seems to delve into my soul. I know he was worried about me during the fight, but it's only now I realize how worried I was about him. If one of those hideous things had killed him today, I don't know what I would do.

I need to tell him! It feels urgent that he know my feelings for him right this minute.

I step next to him so closely it's a miracle any water can slide between us. Looking up into his beautiful face, I grab his cheeks and force his gaze to mine. "I love you Bayne. I love you and don't want to lose you."

He smiles. It's not a big, beaming, dramatic smile, but the sweetest show of upturned lips that screams how happy my words made him. Then his smile widens, giving me a front-row seat to those sexy fangs.

"I love you too, my Willa. Let me show you how much."

His lips slant to mine, sheltering me from the pelting water as his mouth takes mine. I love the warmth of him, his spicy taste, the firm softness of his lips. My body and mind have changed their focus from the adrenaline rush of a life-and-death struggle to the raging hormones of desire.

My pricked nipples graze his chest as I pull him to me, my hands roaming his back. I love foreplay, and goodness knows, he's so very good at it. But I need none now.

Reaching between us, I capture his hard cock and stroke. Over the past few days, I've explored his cock, but it still fascinates me. It has three distinct parts, like three bulges stacked on top of each other. I never got my mouth past the second part, but it strikes me now that all three of those are going to be inside me in a matter of minutes. I'm not certain he'll fit. But one thing I do know, we'll work it out.

I slip to my knees, my hands following slowly, sliding down the hills and valleys of his ripped chest, along masculine hips, and now grasping his muscular thighs.

I love his spicy, almost cinnamon taste, but barely snatch a taste because the water is streaming down on us. My tongue circles his head. In bed, I like to do this lazily, but there's nothing lazy about what's happening now. My tongue is swift and on a mission.

Perhaps what happened on Fairea is still playing in my head, because I feel a frenzied need to stay focused on this moment—here with Bayne.

I glance up to see him watching me and find my inner exhibitionist as I exaggerate every lick and swirl of my tongue. I add background music to my little show by moaning. His hands lodge in my hair as he shutters his eyes and tips his head back.

I love him in this pose—the powerful gladiator reduced to weakness by a woman on her knees. His Adam's Apple is prominent, his rounded chin pointing upward, and his hips making little thrusting movements.

Seeing him like this fuels my excitement. Although water's sluicing over me, I'm sure my core is wet enough with my own lubrication to accept him right here in the shower.

Cupping his balls, I plunge onto him in one swift motion, my lips getting as far as the valley between the second and third bulge. I've discovered a really sensitive spot here. It wasn't hard to find, it always garners a throaty growl when I flick it with my tongue.

A few more pumps of my head, a few more flicks on his special spot, and Bayne jets into my mouth. His semen is hot and forceful. I love the intimacy of the act.

He slides his hands to my shoulders and pulls me to standing, then lifts me higher until I wrap my legs around his waist. Dipping my head, I lick along the seam of his lips, then press inside his mouth, loving the taste of him, the sexy communion of our wordless exchange.

"I'm going to make love to you, Willa. Come."

He turns off the shower, escorts me out, and grabs a towel to rub me dry. Even though he just came, his cock is hard again, jutting at me, ready. His eyes rake down my body, the look on his face tells me he loves what he sees.

I grab a towel and get to work on him, not wanting to wait an extra second to get to bed. Refusing to wait for him to dry every spot, I grab his towel from him and toss it on the floor where it joins the one I discarded, then pull him into the bedroom.

When we're inches from the bed, I suddenly feel shy. I turn in his arms and stretch on tiptoe to kiss him.

As frenzied as we were moments ago, everything has slowed down and become suddenly serious. He feels it too. His head cocks and his eyebrows lower in question. When he realizes he hasn't spoken his query out loud, he says, "We can wait. We don't have to—"

"We've waited long enough, Bayne. We deserve a medal for waiting. This is going to be amazing."

"You're already amazing," he says. His words are sweet, but the look in his eyes, so warm, so full of love, is even sweeter.

He tenderly lifts me and sets me onto the middle of the bed, then prowls from the foot of the bed on his hands and knees. Splitting me open, his hands on my knees, he's about to put his mouth on me when he stops.

My lids had already shuttered closed, but they pop open to see what stopped his forward motion. He's sitting back on his heels, drinking me in with his gaze.

"You're so beautiful, Willa. I'm a lucky male."

With that, he dips his head, and the time for talking is over. He nips my inner thigh from knee to the seam of my leg. His teeth don't hurt, but they're not particularly gentle. The touch is incendiary. Then he adds accelerant to the fire when I feel the sharp drag of one fang as it traces a fiery path back to my knee and up again. He's careful not to draw blood, but there's something about the danger that he could be slicing me to ribbons that is the ultimate turn-on.

My hands lodge in his soft ruff, then move to the top of his head to clutch there, my thumbs on the velvet of his pointed ears.

I love this part of him. It's his alien aspect, his differences, that remind me of both our distinctions and our similarities.

He bends his head and spears his tongue into me. It's shocking in its intensity, especially because there was no preamble.

"So good, Bayne," I whisper, even though I know so many more good things are in store for me.

He releases a throaty growl, telling me just how good this is for him, too. Then his tongue, so thick and blunt as it pierced my channel, becomes thin and flexible when he points it and swiftly flicks my clit with dedicated precision.

I move my hands to clench the sheets, not wanting to hurt him as my grip tightens with every increment my passion ratchets up.

My hips thrust as I raise my knees, my heels approaching my bottom as I strain to find release. When one finger slides into my wet channel, my orgasm hits, my internal muscles clenching around him.

My ass lifts off the bed and I ride the waves of ecstasy as his fluttering tongue and beckoning fingers milk every last drop of pleasure from my release.

Was it only a few hours ago that I experienced one of the most terrifying moments of my life? Because now I'm relaxed and safe and loved. This moment is made all the more perfect *because* of what happened on Fairea.

I love this male. I love his quiet strength and his protective impulses and his tenderness.

"Make love with me Bayne."

Even with my blatant invitation, he pauses to kiss me, then nips the column of my neck and moves lower to my shoulder. His blunt front teeth scrape the tip of one nipple as his fingers pluck the other. WarDog's close. I can feel it. It's almost as if I can feel him lurking behind Bayne's eyes.

I'm so amped up from what we've already done and what we're about to do that I feel my heart pounding in my clit. My channel is clenching, waiting to be filled.

Bayne switches breasts, his mouth on the other one, stubbornly refusing to take us where we both so desperately want to go. I want to pound on his back in frustration, but I just smile, knowing he delays our gratification in order to make it better.

Finally, I take things into my own hands—literally—by reaching between us and notching him at my channel. He would have to be made of steel to say no to this.

Instead of plunging into me, though, he makes sure our gazes are locked, then drops one perfect kiss on my lips. He slides into me in a slow plunge.

I'm so ready for him, so wet, so primed, but it is still an invasion. I've never been with a male nearly as well-endowed as Bayne. When he gets to his second bulge, he pulses in and out in order to get past the barrier.

It is so deliciously sensual, so arousing, I feel my internal muscles spasming around him. My eyes shock open in surprise. I didn't feel this orgasm coming. It's a delightful mini-climax that is not only pleasurable for me, but milked Bayne's cock to the point he grunts, trying to control his own release.

When my muscles quit spasming, Bayne continues to press into me. His third bulge is bigger than the other two. I never thought he'd fit into me, but we're both determined, and he finally slides all the way in, up to the hilt.

It's tight and rides the razor's edge between pleasure and pain. When he begins rocking his hips against me, my awareness of pain vanishes, and all I feel is pleasure.

I'm swimming in a pool of pleasure—no, bliss. I'm in ecstasy when I feel him pull all the way out and then drive all the way in again. Each bulge provides endless stimulation to the inside of my channel.

He grunts with enjoyment every time he hits bottom. I'm surprised to hear my own moans of contentment, now so loud I imagine they can be heard all the way to the solarium.

He quickens his pace, which puts me over the edge again, my orgasm made even more intense by having his huge cock pressing against my inner walls. He doesn't stop, he just keeps thrusting until I'm having one long orgasm with highs and lows and pauses. It's like a rollercoaster ride with ups and downs but it never lets up.

Everything seems to be building to one final explosion. When it hits, it's so potent, so overwhelming, that a scream rips from my throat. I nuzzle my head to him, somehow finding his shoulder and biting down as my eyes roll into the back of my head in ecstasy.

He growls as his thrusts quicken for that last sprint toward pleasure, then he comes. His jets spurt into me, bathing my internal walls with his hot release. He's a big male—every part of him—but for some reason, he feels even bigger now.

"Um, Bayne?" I don't know how to phrase my question.

"We're knotted. From listening to the other males, it appears it's not common in all races. It will go down soon."

I don't know what evolutionary purpose it serves, but it ensures I'll get my cuddle fix every single time we make love. I like it.

He relaxes on top of me, careful to put his weight on his forearms as he rests his head next to me, his lips on my neck, too tired to pucker. After a moment of this, he kisses me, then flips us so he's on the bottom with me on top. We're still connected.

He wipes stray hair off my face, then rewards me with a grunt.

"High praise," I say.

"Yes. Highest praises."

Oh, the look in his eyes. I think that warm, melty, lovey look in his eyes just might be better than the best-ever-sex-in-the-world that we just had.

"I love you too," I say.

For some reason, I get the feeling that WarDog is close. I don't know how I know, we've never discussed how it actually works inside his head. I know they share the space in there, and I know WarDog is sentient to some extent.

I assume he didn't just pop out now. I imagine he was present for the last hour. This doesn't feel odd, though. It's like a bonus.

"I love you too, WarDog," I say without a hint of awkwardness.

I'm rewarded with a little chuff that sounds so WarDog, yet flies from Bayne's mouth.

"Lucky me," I say with a sigh as I settle into the covers for a well-deserved nap. "When I fell for you I got a twofer."

Chapter Ten

Bayne

This is a new feeling for me. I've never waited to attack an enemy before. Not one intent on killing me. As I explained to Willa, on Skylose the stakes were never death. Which is why we were so completely unprepared and destroyed by the attack on our village that day over ten *annums* ago, we had never had to fight for our lives. We were hunters, not killers. That changes today.

Erro and I are waiting in the forest at our assigned spot. Two other pairs of gladiators are spaced out at the edge of the trees, waiting for the signal. We'll attack here on the ground, and fourteen other males will beam down from the ship at the same time, ensuring the element of surprise.

As we discussed the plan, it was assumed there might be casualties on our end. We all agreed to this mission, though, tired of being on the run. We've been slaves long enough. We want our freedom and are willing to fight for it. The risks and possible sacrifice will be worth it.

Willa is waiting for me on the *Fool's Errand* and I imagine she's more anxious than I am. To her credit, she never begged me not to go. It would have been awkward. As much as I care for her, I couldn't oblige her. I'm a warrior. This is the right thing to do.

It doesn't mean she's not scared for me, though. At least we had last night. I can go to my grave having experienced the love of a good female.

The word "Now!" comes into my ear through my comm. Without hesitation, Erro and I run out of the woods into the open. This will be one of the moments most fraught with danger. We're fully exposed, unprotected.

My heart pounds so loudly I can feel the blood in my ears. When I fought in my canine form, my humanoid self was too buried to feel fear even though I was being led into the arena. Now, I'm aware this moment might be my last. I might never see Willa again.

WarDog whines at that sentiment, *We will succeed. I was undefeated in the arena. We will fight for our mate, avenge our mother, take vengeance for the lives taken from our pack,* he assures me with total canine confidence. I take strength in his conviction.

The fact that we're coming from different directions will make it harder for our enemies to mow us all down, but we have about five-hundred *fiertos* to run before we reach the walls of the compound.

We race silently, not wanting to call attention to our attack. Every *fierto* closer to the compound we get without alerting the guards keeps us all a bit safer. We're over halfway to our destination when our comrades from the ships beam down to join us. It's only now I hear the first laser burst.

Faster, I tell myself, or perhaps it was my canine whispering to me. My strides elongate even as I scan the top of the wall, looking for a target. The males taught me to use a laser this morning. It's an easy concept—point and shoot.

I see the top of a head over the wall and decide not to fire. I don't want to waste ammunition, nor call attention to my location without at least a chance of hitting my enemy.

I hear a cry from my right, knowing one of my comrades has been hit. We went over this in the briefing this morning. We all agreed that stopping for a fallen comrade at this point in the attack would only result in death for both parties. Any males who are hit during the siege will lie as if dead and be picked up after the assault is over.

Miraculously, I'm in the shade of the forty-*fierto* high wall without having been shot at. Most of us are here, at the door. Within a *minima,* Justus has placed explosives at strategic points on the door and blown it. We pour through the opening, weapons at the ready, and fire at anything that moves.

We're all wearing the matching outfits we've made. They are black leather kilts with black sashes and knee-high black boots. We look like a precision army and will be able to tell who is on our own side with the swiftest glance.

Erro's brother, Turk will try to stay out of sight until the fray is over. Barring that, we all know to be on the lookout for a male that looks like Erro. We don't want to accidentally kill the male who helped us plan this.

Two Frains approach from my left. Zar warned us of them, they are hard-shelled bug-type creatures who walk on two legs and are Daneur Khour's preferred muscle. I blast the *drackers* to hell, then forge forward.

More movement comes from my left and I almost shoot an unarmed female who appears to be carrying an armful of clean laundry. Her eyes widen as she tries to scramble backward in fear.

"Hide!" I hiss, certain my rough voice must strike fear through her. "Don't come out until you hear no laser blasts for long *minimas.*" She scurries to crouch behind a dark blue couch.

Without discussion, we split into two cohorts as we search the mansion. The sounds of yelling and fighting drift to me from my right as the other cohort encounters the enemy. A moment later, eight well-armed males halt our movement in a narrow hallway.

Dax, the tallest of us, aims over our heads and mows many of them down with his laser. One is still firing from around a corner. We slip into doorways and peek out, taking shots when we can until we hear the unmistakable sound of a body being hit and then falling to the floor.

Without waiting a moment, we converge in the hallway and continue to sweep the area. Heavy laser fire draws us from the right, and all of my cohort hurries in that direction. I bring up the rear, but something catches my attention. A scent.

My inner canine howls, catching my awareness as if the scent alone wasn't enough to stop me in my tracks. The memory of my mother's head tumbling to the ground flashes through my mind, reminding me of exactly when I first smelled this odor.

Daneur Khour.

I'm on the second floor. I assume behind every door is a bedroom. One of them belongs to the purple bastard who ruined my life. Even if it hadn't been covered in the briefing, I would have guessed Khour would be well-protected and well-armed.

Having no regard for my personal safety, I use my sense of smell to find the male. Pausing at each door, I inhale, then move to the next until I'm certain I've found him.

Enemy. Kill him. Remembering the situation with the vid screen, WarDog uses all his self-control not to burst out of me and through the wooden door. Instead, he steps back to allow me to use my weapon.

Good boy, I quickly praise him.

Checking that I have plenty of charge left in my laser, I press my finger on the trigger and blast through the wooden door into the room from left to right and back again. From the shouts and moans inside I'm certain I've hit more than one enemy.

Stopping to listen, I hear nothing inside. I wait a few moments and then fire another salvo into the room.

The thick wooden door is now obliterated. Shards and splinters are everywhere, including a few lodged in my flesh. Glancing into the room through the still-closed door, I see the charred and burning remnants of a finely-appointed bedroom suite.

I doubt everyone beyond this door is dead, but I'm going in. Using my comm, I call my cadre to give them my location as well as my suspicion that Khour is in this room.

Stepping one foot through the hole I blasted in the door, I scan the room and then enter. One male is in a far corner. It's a purple male of Khour's race—he's badly wounded. Dragging himself by his hands, his legs rendered useless, he's pulling himself toward a weapon.

I'd like to believe this is one of the males who accompanied Khour that fateful day back on Skylose. I'll never know. I don't recall any of their faces, just the one who beheaded my mother. Although I don't have the satisfaction of knowing for certain who I'm killing, I shoot him in the head before he reaches his gun.

All I hear is silence except for the sound of laser fire from far off in the compound.

I see aliens of several races dead on the floor of this bedroom. Four Frains and a shaggy blue male who probably stood seven-*fiertos* tall when he was alive. None of them is Khour.

I pull a six-inch dirk from the scabbard on my thigh and plunge it into the heart of every body on the floor, ensuring they're all dead. My nose tells me Khour has been here within the last *hoara*. In fact, I know he's still here, yet I can't see him.

Is he a sorcerer? A chameleon? Able to turn his body invisible? I stand still and glance around the room, paying attention to subtle clues. Where is his scent coming from?

My attention is drawn to the wall at my left. It's paneled in burled wood made by a craftsman who paid attention to the smallest details. I could swear Khour is behind one of these panels.

I step over bodies to reach the back corner of the room so he won't be able to hit me if he were to shoot through that panel the way I shot through the door.

My heart is pounding, and it has nothing to do with the danger I'm in. It's because I'm so close to Khour. I've dreamed, even in my canine form, of killing this bastard since he slaughtered my village. To be so close and not be able to reach him will drive me insane.

I hear the sound of footsteps pounding down the hallway. Eight of my comrades barge through the doorway after opening the destroyed door.

"Where is he?" Steele asks, his intelligent eyes scanning the room.

"I know he's here, hiding. I believe he's behind this wall."

"My weapon has charge left," Stryker says. "Stand back." As soon as I step out of his line of fire, Stryker lets loose a steady stream of fire. A moment later, when he stops shooting, instead of seeing through the wall into the next room, we see thick metal plating behind what was left of the decimated wooden wall.

"Finish the job, Stryker," Shadow says.

The gladiator continues to fire until there is almost nothing left of the original wood veneer of the wall. We see a shining silver metal wall; it withstood the barrage of laser fire.

"A safe room," Shadow announces.

"What?" Stryker asks.

"My parents had one." An idiot couldn't miss the hatred and disdain with which he says the word 'parents'. "And well they should have. They collected enemies like other people collect jewels. It's a fortified room or closet within a house where the owner can retreat in times like these. See this?" He touches a seam that was hardly visible until he pointed it out. "And this? These seams outline the doorway."

"The *motherdracker* is in there, alright. Hiding like the coward he is," Dax says.

"What should we do? Will Justus be able to blow the door off?" Stryker asks.

"As hated as Khour is, I doubt he spared any expense in constructing this room. We'll try certainly, but I don't think we'll be able to blow our way in," Shadow says. "Steele, Dax, Stryker, and Maximus, wait here while the rest of us secure the grounds. You all have enough ammo?"

They nod.

I don't want to secure the compound. I want to stay here and figure out how to kill my mortal enemy. I'm not in charge, though. I just joined the crew, at least as a humanoid. I catch up with the group as they wander the hallways investigating every bedroom, refresher, and closet along the way.

When the house is secured, we inspect the outbuildings. There are many of them, including a small *ludus* with attached slave barracks. We spend *hoaras* combing through the area, investigating the thick stone walls, the groundskeeper's cottage, and an old stable.

We find Erro's brother Turk in the groundskeeper's cottage with six innocent staff he was protecting. We send them to the mansion.

"Let's rendezvous back in the main quarters in an *hoara*. Each of you go back and cover a sector one more time." Shadow says.

"I'll take the area near the garden," I announce, then hurry over to it. Something just didn't seem right when we investigated it before.

The well is a round, stone structure that looks like it was part of the original grounds that were built centuries ago, long before the mansion was erected. When we passed here before, something nagged at the back of my mind, although I'm not certain what.

Now that I'm here, I see it. I check my laser and see that it's almost back to full charge, then ease forward to the patch of soil behind the well. It's been recently disturbed. The ground hasn't been tamped down properly.

I kick the dirt with my boot and easily scrape it down until I feel something hard underneath. After hurrying to the groundskeeper's shed, I return with a shovel. In just a few moments, I scuff newly-placed earth off a wooden panel, then prise it up and hurl it a few *fiertos* away.

Steps. There are steps hewn into the soil. By the look of it, they've been trod not that long ago. Someone went to great lengths to hastily cover this over and hide its existence.

I hurry down the steps with a sense of urgency. It's not just my instincts that are blaring an alarm, but my canine is chuffing inside, by his impatience this mission seems urgent.

My nose is assailed with smells. None of them are good. The first thing I notice is the stink of dirty bodies. The filth is so thick, the stench so horrendous, I'm not sure if I'm smelling animals or humanoids. Even WarDog drops and covers his nose with his paws.

Then the scent of misery slams into me like it's a living thing. Fear and dread vie with anger for my most prevalent emotion.

I'm in a dungeon under the soil. It's almost pitch black in here. There are dim lights built into nitches in the walls. Even with them, it's almost too dark to see my hand in front of my eyes. I smell death, or perhaps dying. That's clear. But there are living souls here too. Humanoid.

Cells are crammed in down here. Old, rusting bars not just on three sides, but on four, so the poor souls couldn't claw their way out through the dirt wall at the rear of their cells.

I swallow. Hard. But it's not enough to keep my emotions at bay. Tears warm my eyes as I see the misery here. Naked males of many alien species. They're filthy. And there are no facilities. The buckets of shit and piss are overflowing. WarDog whines in misery.

We were kept in a cell just like this.

Thank the Gods I don't remember this, WarDog. Though I'm sorry I wasn't there to help you shoulder the burden.

The water buckets in each cell are empty, and when I see the inhabitants' parched lips, I have no doubt they haven't had a drink in far too long.

The most surprising thing of all is the silence down here. Where are their pleas? Why aren't they welcoming me as their rescuer? Or at least questioning me about who I am and why I'm here?

I know the answer before I ask, though. Fear. These males are terrified. They all sit on bunks whose mattresses were eaten by vermin long ago. Their eyes are downcast, their emaciated shoulders slumped. None of them have the courage to look at me. None have kenned to the fact that I'm not their usual jailer. Maybe this isn't fear I smell but despair. Total hopelessness.

"I'm Bayne," I say, trying to imbue my voice with friendly confidence. "I've come with a cadre of males to free you." Surely they heard the weapon fire. But no, down here in the depths of the soil they would have heard none of the life-and-death battle we waged up above.

"I'm Bayne from the ship the *Fool's Errand*. Our ship and the *Devil's Playground* have come to set you free. We've killed all of your captors except Daneur Khour himself. We'll be coming up with a plan to do that before the sun sets."

I watch as one by one the males hazard a glance at me, then look down at their feet again. Now that my eyes are better accustomed to the darkness, I see some of the remnants of their physical pain—whip marks, bodies so thin I can count the ribs, lips cracked and white from thirst, and evidence of vermin bites in every stage of healing.

If I hadn't wanted to kill Daneur Khour before I descended into this hole, I certainly do now.

"Urgent!" I call into my comm. "I need a cohort of males to the well. As many as can safely be spared. I've found prisoners. Come with water and blankets. Some of these captives won't be able to walk out of here without help."

I don't have to look far for the keys. It's as if they were placed by a sadist. The ring of keys is large, hanging on the wall across from the cells so every prisoner could look at it all day long knowing he'd never reach it, never taste freedom again.

I don't know if I've ever felt so relieved as when I hear the first boot strike the top step. Soon my males, my comrades, are here, offering water and covering filthy naked bodies with the first coverings they've worn in . . . I have no idea how long.

I'm proud to be part of this. I'm a liberator. A helper. I found these males who certainly would have died within days if I hadn't stumbled onto this secret hiding place.

None, not one of these males has the strength to walk up the steps on their own power. My hands fist at my sides and I have an inner battle with my canine to calm him. He's throwing himself at me, trying to burst out and shift. He desperately wants to help. I only help him gather control when I tell him it would traumatize many of these prisoners to see me turn into a fighting canine with two-inch teeth.

He pulls back, but just a bit, watching with so much anger and sorrow I know he'd kill Khour with his bare teeth if he ever got the chance.

My comrades have emptied the dungeon, and I look around one last time to see if perhaps one of the males had one possession, a piece of clothing perhaps that he might want to carry out of this heinous place, although I can't imagine any of them will want a memento to remember this place by.

This primitive place had a walkway that held only the keys on the wall. Across from it were eight cells, now empty, thank the Gods. The dim lighting was only near the steps. At the eighth cell, it's close to pitch black.

I see a small mound of . . . something on the floor of the last cell. The remnants of a rat-eaten mattress? A pathetic piece of blanket the male used to cover himself with? My eyes give me no additional information, but my nose tells a different story.

I smelled death when I entered this forsaken place. Here's a body. I say a prayer for the poor male who died alone in this Godless place.

My inner canine whines to get my attention. *Wait.* When I follow his intuition, I see the slightest movement. Could something be alive here?

I open the cell and approach slowly. Whatever, whoever, is here might be frightened of me.

"I'm Bayne," I croon as if I'm talking to a scared pup. "I've come to rescue you." I'm still not sure if I'm talking to a male, a pile of rags, or a dead body.

It's definitely alive. I see the shallow movement of breathing, though I'm still not sure what manner of creature my eyes are seeing.

I crouch down and move the rags, but they're not rags, it's fur. When I look closely, then sweep fur from his face, I see a male of Zar's race. The light is dim, but what I see is enough to turn my stomach.

The male has the flat feline face that's similar to the captain of my ship. His lips are pulled back in a rictus of pain exposing two empty spots where his fangs should be. Did someone pull this male's teeth? Of course. It would render him more defenseless, although it's hard to look at him now and believe he could ever have been a threat to anyone.

His fur is coming out in tufts, from malnutrition I assume. His muscle tone is nonexistent. He could no more sit up than a babe right out of his mother's womb.

Even with immediate medical attention, I wonder if he will live another *hoara* above ground.

"Zar!" I comm excitedly. "I know we agreed you should stay on the ship and not be in the melee, but you need to come down here. If Dr. Drayke isn't saving a life, he needs to bring a stretcher and medkit. Tell Willa I'm fine, not to worry. I'm in the dungeon near the well in the courtyard.

I stay crouched near the male and scrutinize his features. He's panting, his tongue lolling between his lips. His fangs are conspicuous in their absence. His head is too weak to lift, but his golden eyes watch my face. I walk to an abandoned water bucket Erro brought down, grab the dipper, and bring it to this dying male's lips.

He's too weak to drink, so I drizzle a few drops of water onto his tongue. He opens his mouth for another sip, and then another. The moment Shadow joined us down here he warned us not to introduce food or drink too quickly to these males. Unbelievable as it sounded, he assured us it could actually kill them.

"I'll give you more in a moment, my male. Just one sip at a time though." I touch his shoulder. Just the barest touch. The male's muscles twitch, as if he's trying to flinch but doesn't have the strength. I wonder how long it's been since he's felt a touch not filled with torment.

I'm certain he can't talk, and wonder if he even has a translator. But I babble to him, hoping that by my presence he knows help has arrived.

"We've got an excellent physician," I tell him. "We'll nurse you back to health on our ship." Even as I say these words, it feels like I'm lying. He's too far gone. I fear I interrupted his dying breaths. Certainly, if he had any fight left in him, indeed, any *life* left in him, he would have called out before the last one of us walked up the steps and abandoned him here to die alone.

It seems like an eternity before I hear footsteps. Zar bounds down the steps, followed by blue Dr. Drayke.

"Here," I say, assuming they're still blinded by the change from the bright outdoors to the darkness down here.

Zar approaches, certainly knowing something remarkable must be happening. No one would have called him here unless it was an extraordinary circumstance.

It takes him a moment, as it did me, for his mind to make sense out of what his eyes see. I stand and move out of the way to allow him access to his fellow countryman.

"Ton'Arr," he says as if it's a prayer. "Ton'Arr," he intones more loudly. This is the name of his race.

I've backed into the corner, but I can see the male's face. The dim light allows me to see his eyes widen, then fix on Zar's face. He makes a pitiful sound. It's unintelligible. My translator works fine. I doubt his lips do, though. But he tried to speak. Perhaps there's hope for him yet.

Zar's feline features look fearsome when he's serious. Even when he's jovial, but especially when he's somber. Right now I can tell he wants to kill whoever is responsible for this.

"Drayke!" He calls the doctor, his voice hoarse with emotion.

"Right here, Zar."

I watch as the doctor bustles in and tends the male on the floor. After running a battery of tests on his medpad, he pulls out a vial and attaches it to his hypogun.

"I'm going to inject you with a stabilizer to strengthen your heart so we can get you out of here," he softly tells his patient. The male blinks his eyes, too weak to even move his head. After injecting him in the side of the neck, Dr. Drayke consults the medpad, then pronounces it safe for the male to be carried up top where the stretcher awaits. The steps were far too steep to bring the stretcher down here.

I kneel to pick up the male, not wanting my captain to be sullied by this poor male's matted hair and fetid skin. Zar shakes his head. I can see the tears in his eyes. Somehow by his proud bearing and the look on his face, I wonder if he considers it an honor to tend to his countryman. Perhaps it will be the last act of kindness this poor devil will ever experience.

It's with the utmost care, as if he's touching his race's most sacred religious book, that he hefts the male into his arms, one forearm under the male's back, one in the crook of his knees. Hugging the male to his chest, he strides to the steps and takes them slowly, not wanting to jostle the dying being in his arms.

The male groans when they reach the sunlight. I imagine the light, which he hasn't seen in *annums*, must sting his eyes. When I reach the top step, Zar is standing so his shadow falls across the male as the doctor straps him to the hover-stretcher. The male groans in relief.

"Join the others on the main floor of the mansion. They're having a meeting," Zar tells me, then beams up to the *Fool* with his charge and the doctor.

Chapter Eleven

Willa

"Um, your attention please." It's Anya's voice over comms. The pit of my stomach feels like it's being bathed in acid and squeezed in a tight fist at the same time.

In the moment between the end of her sentence and the beginning of the next, my mind flies to visions of a thousand terrible things she's about to announce. The one that circles round and round in my head is that she's telling us they've all been killed. Or at least my Bayne has.

As I picture him lying dead on that awful planet, tears spring to my eyes.

"The fight is going well. Their report is that all the enemy has been vanquished except Khour."

I sigh in relief, more thankful even than when the *Fool's Errand* rescued us from the slaver ship.

"Only one serious injury. Wrage. He's already bellowing to be released from medbay, so I wouldn't worry too much about him. You can wish him well later. I'll put even odds on whether he's even still in medbay or not. But ladies, we have more important things to do."

As I pay attention I look at the comm unit in my ceiling as if the speaker is a vid unit.

"The males found a group of women in an outbuilding on the property. They barged in, secured the perimeter, and are staying at the periphery until we arrive, believing the presence of a bunch of huge gladiator males would traumatize them.

"We're already in the process of treating some malnourished and abused males we found in a dungeon. I'm not certain what shape these females are in."

I drop onto the bed, my legs giving out. The extent of cruelty I've encountered during my sojourn in space is staggering. Abused males, traumatized females. Thank goodness I'm safe now. And I've found Bayne. I quell my rising fear by assuring myself Anya would have told me if something had happened to him.

"I'm looking for volunteers to go down to the planet with me to meet these females, assess what's going on, and provide assistance."

I hit my comm immediately, "I'm in," I say although I don't know what help I can be. Within moments I'm dressed and waiting near the transporter with five other women.

They transport us to what appears to be a courtyard in the middle of the compound. The mansion is to my back, an old well is in front of us, and to the side is an old building that reminds me of a two-story college dorm. It's quaint and utilitarian.

Steele greets us, then accompanies us to the building made of the same chestnut and gold stone that constructs the whole compound.

I didn't notice at first, but the charming old-fashioned building has something most college dorms don't—bars on the windows. We enter onto a common area where the males have evidently rounded up all the females.

I'd expected to see a variety of alien females, but it sure looks like a bunch of Earth girls.

"Earth?" Anya asks without preamble.

They all nod, eyes wide. They must be as surprised to be rescued by a bunch of Earth girls as we are to find them.

It doesn't take long to discover these five women were being held against their will, most were awaiting sale. It never ceases to amaze me that although humans are prohibited in space, the slave traffickers seem to prefer us. I was told it's because our genetics are bland and it's easy for just about any species to breed with us and produce offspring that look like the father.

The women seem to be in good physical shape. At least the asshole kept them fed. The doctor is busy with the malnourished males they found on site, but when he has time, he'll give all the women a thorough exam.

"You're free to leave this building," Anya tells them after consulting with Zar, her mate. "I don't recommend it. The grounds are littered with dead males—the ones who kept you prisoners here. We'll have to meet to decide what to do, but you're free and we'll ensure you all wind up in a good place."

"How soon can you get us back to Earth?" a small woman with tight brown curls asks.

"You'll wind up in a good place," Anya says as she shakes her head sadly. "It won't be Earth. Humans don't want to know there are other species out there capable of space flight. If you went back they'd take you directly to a place like Area 51 and your life would be miserable—that is if they don't dissect you."

The look of hope on every single face is dashed, shoulders sag. I'm sure Anya hates being the bearer of bad news as much as these women hate to hear it.

I sit on a couch between a blond and a brunette and try to lend a comforting hand.

"It's not so bad," I tell them. I think of how miserable I was at first, and how happy I am now that Bayne and I have found each other. "Sometimes you don't even have to work hard to make lemonade out of lemons."

Bayne

The gladiators are in the living area of the mansion which is now riddled with dead bodies and the charred evidence of laserfire.

"The house staff have been rounded up and are in a room waiting to be interrogated," Shadow begins the moment I walk through the archway. "We'll make certain they're innocent, then release them. We've combed the area and believe we've neutralized all Khour's henchmen.

"We've located and are treating eight males we found in an underground dungeon. We've found some females we believe are from Earth and will be deciding what to do with them.

"Follow me," he says as he walks through the front door and out into the courtyard where we have to step over two bodies. We continue to follow until we're in the open area between the house and trees, about one hundred *fiertos* from the house.

"Khour is a rich and powerful male, and never to be underestimated. I'm certain he has surveillance cameras throughout the house, but doubt he can hear us all the way out here. I know what this male is capable of. He was my parents' employer for a while, right before he convinced them to throw me into slavery to pay their debt to him. I hate the *motherdracker* with every breath I breathe."

My belly tightens with this information, reminding me just how much I loathe the male. More than one of us in the group has reason to want to kill him.

"His panic room is most likely equipped with enough food and weapons to outwait us. We can't stay here forever waiting for him to come out of his room."

We include Zar and Beast via comm and discuss ways to lure him out for the better part of an *hoara*. I picture Khour sitting in a comfortable suite of rooms with plush seating and a refresher fit for a king. He probably has not only fine food, but a selection of his favorites spirits. He's got vids and satellite feed, and is watching us huddle out here trying to outsmart him. He's probably chuckling to himself believing he's outwitted us.

We come up with nothing that will work and are trying to wrap our heads around the fact that we'll be leaving this planet without the male we came to kill, although we put a good dent in the cartel's ranks by dispatching over thirty of their soldiers. Only Wrage was injured in the attack, and Dr. Drayke says he'll make a full recovery.

The conversation is winding down. We've thought of every eventuality and don't know how to coax him out. We can't wait forever. During the entire conversation I've known exactly what I'm going to do, I've just waited for the group to run out of options before I suggest it.

"I'm staying," I announce brashly.

"What?" Dax asks, his head whipping toward me. "What would that accomplish?"

"Let's make a show of leaving. The males from the dungeon are already on the ship. The *Fool's Errand*, right? That's where Dr. Drayke is."

Shadow nods.

"Make sure Khour sees us parade the females through the house. We'll land the *Devil's Playground* right here in his front yard. There's room there for all of them, right?"

Erro nods. He resides on that ship.

"He'll watch all of you fly away after we have a loud discussion right outside his room about giving up and having other more urgent things to do. Doesn't someone have an important gladiatorial match they must attend?

"I will have quietly wandered into the woods. Before you go, I can set up surveillance vids in what's left of his bedroom and can sneak back when he opens his hideyhole."

"Then what?" Stryker asks.

"I kill the *motherdracker*," I seethe.

"No," Shadow says with finality at the same moment I hear Zar and Beast say the same thing through the comm. "Suicide mission."

"Khour's well-armed," Zar says.

"I'll have a surprise." I allow WarDog to growl for emphasis.

"I don't condone it," Zar's voice is firm. Beast grunts his agreement.

"With all due respect, Zar, I'm not asking your approval."

"What about your female?" Shadow asks. "You may be willing to put yourself at risk, but will your female be able to tolerate losing you?"

My shoulders slump as a fist squeezes my heart. As much as I want to kill Khour, I know this is a suicide mission. Can I really do this to Willa?

"She's in the dormitory?" I ask, having heard a contingent of our females came down to help the ones we liberated.

"Yes, it's past the well to the north," Dax says.

"Don't make any decisions without me. I'll be back," I say as I stalk off.

Just walking by the hole in the ground near the well and seeing the rough-hewn steps that led to the hellhole we discovered underground makes bile rise in the back of my throat and my nostrils flare with the remembered stench.

WarDog's hackles rise and he growls. *Find him. Kill him.*

Easy boy, I want that as much as you do. We have to talk to our mate. WarDog immediately stands down and I can sense the same anticipation and trepidation I feel as I swiftly seek out Willa for the conversation that awaits us.

I hurry, and moments later I call Willa through the arched front door. I don't want to enter, it might traumatize the females. Who knows what has been done to them in this forsaken place?

Willa runs through the doorway, across the covered porch, and into my embrace, almost tackling me. After throwing her arms around me, she peppers my face with kisses and then leans back to inspect me.

"Oh my God, where are you hurt?"

I shake my head. "Nowhere."

"You have blood everywhere." Her fingers gently wipe my face.

Raising my hands I look down to inspect down my body. "No injuries. That's the blood of others." I recall one of the Frains I killed when we first breached the front door. His arterial blood sprayed everywhere.

She sags into my arms again, her hands roaming my back as if to ensure every part of me is unharmed.

"We need to talk," I tell her, my voice grim.

Every muscle in her body tightens. The way I said those words was a clear message that what's coming next is not going to be good.

As I explain the predicament and my plan, she seems to cave in on herself as if her frame is shrinking the longer I talk.

"A suicide mission, Bayne?"

Her tone is doleful. She has to be thinking how terrible the timing is. We just found each other, and now I'm walking into a likely death trap.

She hugs me so tightly it's like she wants to crawl into my skin with me. She's quiet, thinking. Finally, she says, "I know how much you hate him."

"Yes."

"He killed your mother."

"Yes." Her mind is thinking this through, gaining an understanding of what I'm going through.

"He set in motion the events that trapped you in canine form for a decade."

"Aye."

"I imagine it would be torture for you to walk away from him, from this opportunity to kill him."

"Yes."

"I'm trying to figure out which one of us would be in more agony," she says, obviously using every scrap of self-control she has to manage her grief. "Would it be you if you walk away and let him live, or me if you die on Fairea and I never see you again? I think the torture would be about equal."

"Probably, Willa." I pull her to me even more tightly and rub her back while I nuzzle her hair. In my mind, WarDog is emitting a constant whimper as Willa's overwhelming scent of fear, grief and love envelop us. It's breaking our heart but I hold firm.

"You know I don't want you to do this," her gaze spears mine, "but I understand, Bayne. I do. I won't give you my blessing—you'll never get that. And I won't give you permission, that's something parents give their children; we're equals in this relationship. But I will give you compassionate forgiveness. I understand."

My heart squeezes knowing just how much her generosity is costing her. "Thank you, Willa. I love you. With all my heart. Forever and always." I sag with relief and let out the breath I was holding.

WarDog stops the heartrending sound he was making but is still on his belly with his head on his paws and his ears tipped back, overwhelmed by Willa's fear. I regret only one thing right now. I should have made her my mate the other night when we made love.

Maybe, though, it's a blessing. Since we're not mated, if I die she'll be able to move on, find someone else. That thought makes me feel as though someone threw a spear through my heart.

My inner beast leaps to his feet, standing tall and proud and declares *We will not fail. We will find our enemy. Kill him. Return to our mate and claim her.* Although I'm relieved to have my partner solidly behind me, I know our chances of succeeding are still uncertain.

Pressing my lips to her ear I decide to decimate any barriers that might still be erected between us. I might never see her again. I want to give her this, a final gift. She can carry my words with her in her heart even if we never see each other again.

"I love you, my Willa. As much as any male ever loved any female. When I was a youngling tales were told around the fire at night. My favorite was of the sun god and moon goddess who were punished by others in the pantheon of gods. They were forever doomed to never touch, and to only see each other at magical times. Their love for each other never dimmed, though.

"I love you that much, Willa. Keep it with you always. Shining in the darkness. Never doubt it. Never."

She presses her cheek against my chest, hiding her face from me, although she can't hide her tears. I feel them. I smell them.

"I love you, too, Bayne. Whatever happens, know that."

She reaches on tiptoe to kiss me. Not a passionate kiss that would be more fitting in the bedroom, but a sweet kiss filled with all the love and longing two people can have for each other.

Compassionate forgiveness. Only Willa could be so generous when her heart is breaking. I walk away and forbid myself to look back. My inner canine is whining, *Can't leave our mate, need her, love her. We'll kill our enemy. Will come back to Willa.*

It's hard enough without his emotions flooding me, but his heart is breaking, too. I embrace his determination and shore up my own flagging spirit as I walk away from Willa, forbidding myself to look back.

Chapter Twelve

Bayne

The group packs up, stealing everything that isn't nailed down or already smashed to bits. Our females double-check that the rescued females are comfortable with the plan to lodge them onboard the ship, at least for the time being.

While they're doing that, I check out the garage and disable every hover and space vessel in the hangar. Khour isn't going to get off this planet alive. By all the Gods, I vow it.

In all the chaos, with people coming and going, it's easy for me to hide loaded weapons in every nook and cranny of the main mansion. My mind runs hundreds of scenarios, and I plan for every possible disaster that Zar, Beast, and I could conceive. When they found out Willa hadn't persuaded me to abort this mission, they stepped up to help me plan. These are males I am proud to know and call friends.

Khour will come out shortly after everyone leaves. I know it. He's too cocky. Too self-assured. Surreptitiously, I set hidden vid cameras, the humans call them bugs, around the mansion and will see him on my comm the moment the door to his safe room slides open.

Assuming Khour is watching, Willa and I can't bid each other a proper goodbye. He'd catch in a minute that something is amiss. Why would we be kissing, why would my female be crying if we were both about to board the same vessel?

She knows my feelings—I told her. She knows she owns my heart. And I know my feelings are returned—like a mated pair.

"Willa. When I see you again . . ." I purposely don't say the word 'if'. "When I see you again, will you be my mate?" I said this in a husky whisper directly into her ear.

Her eyes catch mine and she tries with all her might to smile at me, but sadness is etched on her features. "I don't know what that means, Bayne. But if it means I get to have you and perhaps your canine around all the time, then yes. Yes, I'll be your mate. It would make me happier than just about anything in the galaxy."

She doesn't have to say what would make her even happier—for me to leave with her on the *Fool's Errand* right now.

We walk in a group to the empty field between the front door and the treeline. In all the chaos, I make my way to the trees as the group board the *Devil's Playground* or beam aboard the *Fool.*

As the sun sets, I realize that although I'm armed with lasers now, if the tarantu-scorps, as Willa calls them, attack me, I'll either be cut to bits by their sharp pincers or will have to use my laser. If so, my cover will be blown and I might as well beam up to the *Fool*, Khour will never appear if he knows I'm out here waiting for him.

I climb a tree, lodge my back against the bark, my ass in the crotch between a limb and the trunk, and watch my comm.

I turn my volume all the way up, having placed bugs that transmit audio and video in what was left of his room. If that panel slides open, I'll hear it and sneak back to the house.

Realistically, I know I might have to wait days. I believe males like Khour, full of power and bluster when they have a phalanx of armed males around them, are often fearful when they're left to their own devices. He might be cowering in his panic room. But somehow I doubt that.

I'm shocked when I'm awakened in the middle of the night by the screech of metal on metal. My eyes fly open and I watch as the hidden panel in Khour's room slides open and the lavender male himself strides out.

A picture of him as a younger male flashes into my mind. He may have been younger, but he was full of self-importance even back then. No, self-importance isn't the correct word. He was cocky. Even then his eyes were dead.

But I recall he was handsome. Once I got over my astonishment at seeing an alien for the first time, I could appreciate his looks. Straight nose, compelling yellow eyes, strong physique—females would be attracted until his eyes revealed he had no soul.

He's nothing like that now, though. Ruined. It's the only word that can describe what I see on his face. It's so repulsive I'm fascinated. I watch him from different angles as he walks from one camera's frame to another. His skin has the consistency of clotted milk in some places and dripping wax in others.

They said the pirate Sextus carved initials into his face then threw acid on it. I can't read the writing, but I can see someone wrote something there. How that must enrage him every time he looks in the mirror! Although with that face, I doubt he looks into the mirror much.

"I'm going in," I speak into my comm, then climb to the ground and watch Khour's vid stream, waiting until he makes his way through the carnage. He travels from room to room, seeing the remains of his males, noticing his precious items either smashed or stolen. I hope he feels the loss of his things as much as I felt the loss of the people I loved.

Don't worry, dracker, *you won't feel miserable for long. You'll be in hell soon enough.*

Kill, WarDog says on a deep growl.

Khour is in his living room now. Although it's hard to read emotions on his ravaged face, I can tell he's not happy by the way his lavender skin has turned deep purple. This gives me a shred of satisfaction.

From what I know of this male, I doubt his distress is about the people who used to work for him who are now lying dead on his floor. I imagine it's more about the destruction of his property, or the fact that no one is left in his compound to clean up his mess.

He's distracted and near the front door. Now is the perfect time to strike. I bound across the open space between the tree line and the front door. My muscles strain to get there quickly. WarDog is close to the surface, urging me to go faster. He wants this as much as I do.

My laser pistols are in my hand, fully charged. It would be the work of a moment to barge through the front door and slice him in half with a long laser burst, but I can't force myself to do that. I've yearned for revenge for too long. I want to make him hurt, to make him pay for what he did to me and every other being he has killed, enslaved, and tortured without a shred of conscience. Not to mention all the families he has destroyed. I am doing this for all of us.

The door was decimated upon our entry earlier; Justus's explosive charge did its job. I slow my pace so Khour doesn't hear my approach, sneak onto the front porch, and burst through the opening, weapons drawn.

Khour was stooped over and now rises with half a white porcelain statue in his hand. He doesn't seem especially surprised to see me. Has he set a trap? Why would he be so casual when a huge armed male burst into his house?

"I'm a wealthy male," he says, barely giving me a glance. "I'll make it worth your while to spare my life."

This is so odd, not at all what I expected. Where is his fear? The begging and pleading I've imagined every day I've walked on two feet since he killed everyone in my village? Is he so used to buying every being he comes in contact with?

"I care nothing for your credits, nor your trinkets," I scoff and brandish my guns.

"A job?" he asks as he stoops to retrieve something.

"Stand!" I order.

He shrugs, then points to the jagged piece of statue he holds in his hand. It's the top half of a white porcelain female. "What are tits without a cunt?" he asks, his thoughts as coarse as I imagined they'd be.

"You're broken." The thought flew out of my mouth before I knew it.

"Oh, this?" he casually waves at his face. "From an enemy. A little gift to remember him by."

"Your brain," I answer. "Your brain is *dracked*." Why am I talking to him? Why are we talking at all? Why isn't he either drawing a weapon if he has one or trying to talk his way out of his imminent death?

"Go ahead then." He shrugs. "Put me out of my misery."

He bends to retrieve the bottom half of the statue, and I shoot, aiming for his heart. He's right. I should end this.

After firing my laser I somehow wind up feeling the searing pain of the shot myself. It throws me back five *fiertos* and I land painfully on my ass. The scorching agony fries my brain's circuits for a moment before I can think clearly.

Khour is still sifting through the remains of his artwork in shards on the floor. I shake my head, trying to make sense of what just happened.

I shot Khour and the laser burst arced back at me, hitting me in my chest just below my shoulder. Thank the Gods the power of the shot somehow reduced on the return trip. The ricochet of what would have been a killing shot to Khour only wounded me. There is a burn mark with the smell of singed fur and skin but little blood. I stand, sway a bit, then shake my head to bring myself back to the moment.

Let me help, WarDog offers. *I can kill him.*

I need to do this.

"Surprise!" he goads, still giving more attention to the rubble on the floor than to me. "My panic room was well equipped. I have to say, I didn't expect you to come barging through my front door, but I was distracted and forgot to remove my body armor, so I'm well protected."

My fingers tighten around the handle of both pistols as I parse through the facts. I want to shoot the *dracker* again, but am pretty sure the next shot will ricochet back at me too. One or two more shots like that and I'll be lying in a smoldering pile of ash and Khour will still be standing amid the debris.

"Weapons won't work against me," he says with a shrug. "Very fancy body armor made by artisans on Abachae. Designed so lasers bounce back to their point of origin. I'm a big male and would be happy to go hand-to-hand with you. I practice daily with the best trainer money can buy. I'll win."

His taunts make me more determined to make him suffer. I consider hitting him with a headshot because I'm fairly certain no protective armor protects his head. I immediately discard the thought of a swift death for the monster standing smug and confident in front of me.

I toss my weapons to the ground. What was it one of the females said when we were planning this in the *ludus*? 'Revenge is a dish best served cold'? She was right. Killing him up close will be much more satisfying than at the unfeeling barrel of a gun.

Now, WarDog growls, his lips are pulled back in a display of savagery, his deadly incisors dripping in anticipation. *Let me at him.*

The depth of his hatred seeps through to me, magnifying my own.

I only feel a small percentage of the desire he feels to attack. It's powerful.

Keep the element of surprise for a moment longer, I urge, wanting to prolong the joy of finally achieving my long-awaited revenge.

I rush Khour with a yell. Bridging the distance between us in a few steps and a leap, I'm relieved to realize that whatever his body armor is capable of, it doesn't repel me. I should have been smart enough to anticipate the stab of the sharp shard of the statue, though. It was still in his grip. He's used it to punch into my stomach, piercing a gouge into me at least three *inces* deep.

I scream in agony and take a step back, indicating I'm in even more pain than I am. I'm less than two *fiertos* from him, able to see every emotion that crosses his evil face. He planned this. He wanted me to think he was distraught and defenseless, he drew me in all the while keeping the deadly, jagged piece of statuary that he could use as a weapon. He's a smart male. I curse myself that I fell for his ploy.

Look at his smug face. He's not even breathing hard and I'm spilling blood all over his formerly fine carpet. If I was a regular humanoid I believe he'd have dealt me a mortal blow. Or, if not this slash, then the next.

I'm not a normal humanoid. I carry a secret, too.

If I was as badly wounded as I'm feigning, I'd be unable to attack him. As it is, though, I don't have much time. If I wait much longer, I'll bleed out before striking my first blow.

We're close. Because I'm panting in pain, I'm certain he can feel the warm puffs of my breath. I'm not worried. Shifting to my canine form will accelerate my healing. I know the bleeding will stop and the wound will begin to close after the shift.

Yes, WarDog coaxes.

When I was out of control and shifted in the dining room, I resented him. I welcome him now, though. It feels comfortable to be back in his huge body. Maybe it's because he will feel my wounds as my body becomes his and he will bear the brunt of the pain of the puncture and laser wounds.

Mostly, it's because we're a pair, he and I. We work best as a team. As I admit this to myself and feel the soul-deep rightness of this conviction, the anger, resentment, and jealousy I have been harboring toward him melt away leaving me feeling strong. It is with renewed determination I tear down the barriers I put between us and fully reconnect with my inner beast.

I watch Khour closely as my body suddenly morphs painlessly to my other form, my more deadly form. For the first time, I see fear on the purple male's features. That's right, *drackhole*, see these teeth?

WarDog growls, deep and low—sheer four-legged menace. He pulls back his lips just to heighten the effect. These teeth are going to be ripping your disgusting flesh off your face in a moment. But first, let's teach you there's a new level of pain you've never dreamed of. Welcome to hell.

It feels good to be in this body—full of power and grace. WarDog eases closer to Khour, pressing him toward the corner. Khour still has the bloody shard in his hand and slashes at WarDogs face. My canine champion of the arena moves a huge paw with lightning reflexes and knocks it from his hand, sending it flying across the room. Now weaponless, Khour's eyes are practically white with panic.

The armor might hurt your teeth, I warn my beast. *Exposed areas only until we're done playing.*

Must you take the fun from everything? he asks as he keeps nudging the male until Khour's back hits the wall.

WarDog places a soft mouth around Khour's neck, just a little hint at what's to come. The sharp fangs tease at the male's tender skin. We feel the carotid pulsing under our tongue. Not only can we hear the high whine escaping Khour's mouth, we can feel the vibrations. He stands paralyzed with fear.

I wish I could talk. I'd love for him to know the reason for his death, to remember the beautiful female from Skylose who lost her head to his evil sword. But that's okay. I imagine his mind right now is scrolling through a litany of reasons why he deserves to die today.

I smell blood. Fresh blood, not from the Frains whose body parts are still scattered around the room, but Khour's blood.

Good job, boy, I tell WarDog, whose fangs have traced two parallel lines deep enough into Khour's throat that blood is seeping down his neck and staining the fabric of his shirt.

WarDog growls louder as he opens his mouth wide, turns his head, and bites Khour's face—his top teeth gouging into one cheek, his bottoms into the other.

I feel his jaws tighten, his powerful muscles contracting as they put so much pressure on Khour that his bones crack.

Khour's hands are gripped in the thick fur around WarDog's neck, frantically trying to pull free. The male is squealing now. I relish the noise. It's the noise a young girl might make when being run down by invaders and dragged into her own bed to be hurt and violated. Only this sound is from a grown male. A male who has inflicted pain from one corner of the galaxy to the other. He's petrified, and WarDog hasn't really even geared up yet.

Smell that? WarDog asks proudly.

Oh yes. Piss. Someone pissed their pants in fear. I wish I could speak, I would love to rub this in, damage his pride more fully. *Make it last, I urge.* I waited too long for this to be over so soon.

WarDog releases his hold on our enemy's face and takes a half-step back. He dips his head, grabs one of Khour's hands, and bites so hard I hear bones breaking and taste blood. I revel in the sound of my enemy's anguished cries, then his shallow breathing as he pants in pain.

"Please, change back. I'm a wealthy male," he's stammering now, though he can barely talk through his crushed face. His lips barely move as he pleads and blubbers, making the blood pouring from his wounds froth in his mouth.

I recall how the pleas of my people did nothing to move his stone-cold heart. "I can give you everything. I know you're in there. Change back and you'll be one of the richest males in the galaxy." It's hard to understand him because of the damage WarDog has inflicted to his face.

Great job, I urge. *Do the other hand. Take your time.*

I'm not a good male. Perhaps I don't deserve the love of a fine female like Willa. A good person would not delight in this. A good male would not be pleading with his canine self to prolong this male's agony. But I *am* taking joy in it. I will never regret this. Never.

WarDog releases Khour's hand and looks at it for a moment before he turns his head to grip the other hand. He looked at it for me. A little present from my more animalistic self, although today I think I'm more of an animal than my canine.

Khour's hand was mangled beyond recognition. It looked like the chopped meat Maddie feeds us. She calls it hamburger.

WarDog grabs the other hand and this time bites more slowly, all the while pricking his ears so we hear the delicious sounds of Khour's high, anguished screams of pain.

As soon as WarDog releases the pressure, Khour tries to sound in control. He even manages to add a sneer to his tortured voice when he says, "I remember your piece of *drack* planet. Is that what this is about? I seem to remember setting a village on fire many *annums* ago. Whichever backwoods primitive male you are, I should have never let you live."

He must realize he can't bribe his way out of this, so he's decided he'll try to injure our feelings with his words. Perhaps he's lost all hope and wants to spur us on to hasten the killing blow to end his suffering.

"As I recall that was a fun day. I remember it well. The smell of smoke in my nose couldn't overpower the stench of your unwashed tribe or the metallic scent of blood. It flowed in rivers, didn't it?"

He must sense that he's gotten to us because he keeps up his stream of verbal shit.

"The silence of the dead and the cries of the dying. Ahh, I remember it as if it was this morning." He sniffs in long and deep, enjoying the memory.

"You lived. I must have sent you to fight in your canine form. Did you think of me often? Perhaps thank me for allowing you to express your animal urges?"

Enough, I tell WarDog. *Show him what painful emotions really feel like,* I urge.

Tell me when we can end this. I could do this all day but I want to get back and mate Willa.

I never would have thought WarDog would be the more level-headed of the two of us, but today he is.

A pang of guilt slices through me. If my inner canine is ready for this to be over, I should be, too. He's right, Willa is waiting, and in my bloodlusted mind set on making this male suffer, I'm prolonging her suffering with every *minima* we're apart.

Okay, I tell him, *get the job done.*

I have to give WarDog credit. He could literally bite the male's head off, or rip his carotid out of his neck and get this over in an instant. Instead, he bites the male's arm where there is no body armor so I can appreciate the male's high, female screams of pain, then WarDog shakes his head like canines do when they have prey in their mouths. He keeps shaking, slamming the wall on either side until the male's body acts more like a ragdoll than a humanoid.

He might not be dead yet, but he's certainly no longer conscious.

WarDog finally lets the body slump to the floor and nudges it with his nose.

Think he's dead? he asks.

Don't worry. I'll make certain of it after I switch back. Before you shift, I have something I want to say.

I feel him edge nearer, his head cocked as he waits.

Apologies. I've resented you. Maybe I was even a bit jealous. You were out for all that time. So long. I lost myself. Then I shifted out and Willa felt more comfortable with you than me. She shared more of herself with you. She seemed to prefer you.

But I don't want that again. Ever. We're a team. I want Willa to be my mate, and I want you to be part of whatever life we create together. I know she loves you, too. I'm sorry. I'll never banish you again.

He heaves a huge gust of air, relaxing perhaps for the first time since Khour stepped out of that hover a decade ago.

I missed you, he says with the full force of his golden eyes staring into mine as we face each other in my mind. *I had to take care of everything when you were forced to hide from me for so long. I had to fight. I had to endure . . . so much. Then you finally shifted back and you shunned me. It hurt. I didn't have you. I didn't have Willa. I was lonely. I'd like for us to be a team again. We work well together.*

With that, we both glance at the dead male not two *fiertos* away. I haven't seen him twitch, or breathe, but as soon as I shift, my dirk will be up to the hilt in his heart just for good measure. Although I'm not sure he has a heart.

And then we'll call the *Fool*. And we'll return to our mate. And although mates shouldn't keep secrets, perhaps we should never tell her just how much we enjoyed what happened in this room. With a huff that sounds remarkably like a laugh, WarDog agrees.

As I shift back, I become painfully aware of where Khour stabbed me with the broken end of a statuette. It hurts like the burning fires of seven hells. *Dracker.*

The pain again slips to the back of my awareness when I allow myself to share WarDog's pride and satisfaction that we fulfilled the promise of revenge we made to our uncle, mother, and friends on that fateful day over ten *annums* ago.

We did it. I say to him.

Of course, we did, he replies as if there was never a shred of doubt. He prances and swaggers inside, pulling a laugh from me even in my weakened state.

My legs can barely hold my weight and I stagger. WarDog whimpers in worry.

Get help, you're hurt, can't fix this.

I pull my knife from my leg holster and stagger to Khour as I leave a thick trail of blood. I'm weak and unsteady on my feet, but I make it to Khour, touch the auto-zip to remove the body armor, and stab his chest over and over, making sure the bastard is dead. If there is a heart in his chest, it's no longer beating.

I have just enough energy to whisper, "Come" into the comm and the world goes black.

Chapter Thirteen

Willa

I'm waiting at the gangway as Stryker and Dax rush Bayne up the ramp on a hover-stretcher. I've been standing here since Zar comm'd and told me Bayne had called for retrieval and only gotten out the word 'come' before the comm ended.

Aerie's been at my side for the last hour, holding my hand because I've lost my mind waiting for them to bring him back to me.

Dr. Drayke is here, medpad in hand, ready to start diagnostics the moment he's onboard.

"Zar!" It's either Axxios or Braxxus's voice over the overhead comm. I can't tell the twin pilots' voices apart. "A fleet of six harriers is coming in fast. As soon as the door closes, we'll launch into hyperdrive."

When the hatch closes, I grab the top bar of the hover-stretcher as we race to medbay. I'm glad I'm holding on when I feel the distinctive lurch as we shift into hyperdrive.

Bayne is pale. And covered in blood. The skin on his chest is charred; some of the pelt high on his shoulders is singed. Worse, though, is the gaping wound in his belly. It's three inches wide with jagged edges and appears to have bled profusely although it's not bleeding now.

I want to ask Dr. Drayke a thousand questions, but one glance at his serious face and his swift fingers flying over his pad tells me it's more important for him to tend to my male than to answer me.

My male. Yes, there it is. Bayne is my male. I love him and he loves me. And bonus! WarDog is a two-hundred-pound lovebug who's a great addition to the mix. The male I love, though, looks like if they don't run faster he'll die of blood loss on the stretcher before they reach medbay.

Dr. Drayke is an amazing male. He's supremely competent and has the kindest bedside manner of any doctor I've ever met. The fact that he's not calmly reassuring me makes my heart race. I've seen him with other males' mates when they've come back on board with an injury from a match. He's kind and unflappable and tells them not to worry.

No comforting platitudes are escaping his mouth now.

Aerie is following us, but Drayke won't let her into medbay.

"I only need essential personnel. And of course you, Willa."

Drayke's mate, Nova is here. She's been training as a nurse. They have a telepathic link and can move so swiftly as the perfect team that it's a joy to watch them. There's no joy today, though. My top teeth nibble my bottom lip as I press my back against the wall to get out of the way and watch Drayke give orders to the medbot while Nova cleans his chest wound.

"The belly's the worst," Drayke says out loud for my benefit. "The laser to the chest isn't serious. Well . . ." he pauses as he checks readings on his medpad, "it *is* serious, but it's the abdominal wound that's the real worry. Internal damage and bleeding could . . ."

Maybe I overrated his bedside manner skills. He did *not* reassure me.

I stand motionless for two hours while the medical team and the medbot do what they can. Bayne's beautiful face is pale and immobile as they rush to patch him up.

About an hour into the procedure, I realized I could hover over his right shoulder and still be out of the way. My fingers lodge into the pelt there. When I used to pet him like this in his canine form I always told myself it comforted him. But that's partially a lie. It gives *me* comfort. My fingers feel at home in his soft fur.

I've been watching Drayke and Nova's expressions. They don't need to talk out loud for me to know they're concerned. Nova's amber eyes are especially expressive. She's not optimistic.

"There's nothing more for us to do right now, Willa," Drayke says. "The bleeding has stopped, the damage has been repaired, and the blood he lost is being replaced. Time will tell. I'll sleep in the lab next door tonight. Why don't you sleep in your own bed?"

"Would *you* sleep in your own bed if Nova was lying on this operating table, Doc?"

He flashes me a small smile. "That's not a hypothetical, Willa. Nova was in my medbay when we first met. I did *not* sleep in my own bed."

They look at each other with the most tender expression. They are so happily mated I used to envy them when I watched them together in the dining room. They can't keep their hands off each other.

"I'll roll a bed in here from one of the other rooms. You can sleep just *inces* from Bayne. I understand."

The sympathetic look he flashes does not inspire optimism.

A few minutes later, they've washed off the blood, covered Bayne in a clean sheet and blanket, and left me here alone with my male. I shove the bed next to his, lie down, and stroke the bare arm nearest me.

I haven't prayed in a long time, but I do now.

Bayne

Awareness rises in my head like the slow dawn of the sun. My first conscious thought is to wonder where I am, then I hear WarDog's persistent chuffing. He's close, sitting stiffly, his worried eyes watching me intently. At the first sign of my waking, his tail thumps and he licks my face with unbridled enthusiasm. Even in my mind, it's warm and welcoming, if somewhat sloppy.

You seem awfully happy to see me. I laugh and pull him close for a fierce hug.

I am. I thought you'd heal faster than you did. I could smell Willa's fear and sorrow, and I could not reach her.

Heal? I release him and look down his body for signs of injury.

Not me, you. Remember Khour? He asks. *The laser? The statue in your stomach?*

It all rushes back to me. The most prevalent feeling isn't pain, but satisfaction as I remember every moment of our battle with Khour. The revenge was a decade in the making. If people across the galaxy knew, there would be tens of thousands of them cheering what WarDog and I accomplished in that living room.

Willa? I ask.

WarDog's tail thumps as he says, *She hasn't left our side since we were transported back on board. She's our mate, right? We need to mate her.*

Yes. We will.

I force my eyes open and see Willa at my right. There she is, sleeping in a bed that's pulled next to mine. I pause, wondering if I should wake her. I know she'd want me to wake her the moment I wake up.

"Willa, my love. Wake up."

Her eyes pop open, and a wide smile replaces her initial startle response. The way she scoots next to me reminds me of the way WarDog wiggles to get closer to her. It's endearing. My heart warms at the happiness in her eyes.

"How are you feeling?" she asks as she feathers a hank of hair off my forehead.

"Fine."

"I'm surprised you're up so soon. Not that long ago, Dr. Drayke wasn't sure you'd make it."

I assumed as much. The look of concern on her face, her brown eyes filled with worry, tells me all I need to know about my condition.

"Skylosians heal fast. If my eyes are open, I'll be fine."

The doctor enters briskly from the adjoining lab, medpad in hand. He hides his initial surprise at seeing me awake, then conducts some readings. After setting the pad down, he grabs another as he says, "Looks like this one's broken. You couldn't have recovered that quickly." He fiddles with the pad, his face looking increasingly amazed, then says, "Speedy recovery is an understatement. Is it a shifter trait? Looks like you've made a full recovery."

He unwraps the bandages on my chest and stomach and shakes his head, his eyebrows lifted in astonishment. "I would love to run more tests to find out what is in your blood or genetics that accelerates the healing." He has that excited look a youngling gets with a new toy.

I shrug. "My species heals quickly."

Drayke performs a few more tests, then says, "I still don't understand what I'm seeing, but at this point, you're just taking up space in my medbay. I can study the results of these tests later. You're fine. Zar asked to see you the moment you woke. Think you can talk if he comes to medbay?"

"Yes, as long as my Willa can stay."

Mate, WarDog insists.

Soon, I reassure him as I gulp down two glasses of water while we wait for Zar.

Within *minimas* both Captain Zar and Captain Beast enter my room and squeeze against the wall across from my bed. The room is small and the two enormous males make it feel even smaller.

"We were relieved to hear you've recovered," Zar says with a smile. I always have to look at his eyes when he wears this expression, not knowing whether he's snarling or smiling. His eyes look genuinely happy to see me. "We want to know what happened on Fairea."

"Willa, would you mind finding me some food? I'm starving," I say when I realize the last thing I want is for her to hear the details of what WarDog and I did in that mansion.

"Sure. I'll leave the room. That's what you're asking, right? Do you really want food?" Out of anyone else's mouth, that would be sarcastic, but she's serious. She called it compassionate forgiveness. I believe she'll be granting it to me often—I'm a lucky male.

"I *am* hungry, Willa. And yes, I'm asking you to leave the room."

"I'll take my time," she says and kisses me without embarrassment in front of not one but two captains. WarDog proudly shifts his weight from paw to paw as we both realize the kiss was a bold announcement of her feelings for me.

As soon as she leaves, I tell the males what happened. The further into the story I get, the more they both nod and smile.

"High five!" Beast says as he steps next to me and puts up his palm. When I look confused, he explains, "Aerie taught me. It's a way of saying 'good job' on Earth."

I slap his palm, enjoying being accepted as an equal.

"We're going to call an all-hands meeting for this afternoon. We'd like you to be there."

"Absolutely."

After they leave, Willa returns with a sandwich. I eat ravenously and finish in *mimimas*. Now I've coaxed her to lie down next to me and we face each other.

Before I can speak, she says, "I was worried, Bayne. First I was terrified when they left you on the planet to deal with Khour alone, then even more so when they brought you back on a stretcher. I promised myself many things while you've been in medbay."

I breathe in her sweet scent and WarDog *inces* closer. He's so bonded to her. Her gentle fingers stroking his fur make his life worth living. Guilt slices through me when I recall how I banished him. I reinforce the promise I made to him and myself that I won't do it again.

Thank you, WarDog says with a happy chuff and perks his ears forward to hear Willa while his tail is thumping in a frenzy of delight and anticipation.

"What things did you promise yourself, Love?"

"That making you and a certain furry someone happy is the most important thing in my life. That if I were lucky enough to have you come back to me I'd never let a day go by where I didn't show you how much I love you both." WarDog's tail is wagging so hard his back end is doing a happy dance. I can't help but smile at his exuberance and joy.

She sees my smile and presses her palm to my cheek. I turn my head to kiss her hand. Then her fingers lodge in the pelt at my shoulders. She loves to pet me there.

"It was selfish of me to stay on Fairea and fight Khour, Willa. I know it terrified you. I—"

"I understand, Bayne. I do. Even though I was terrified I was going to lose you, I'm also proud of you for holding fast to your convictions. You succeeded in ridding the universe of one of its most ruthless and dangerous males.

"He wouldn't stop. He continued to threaten our lives and take away the freedom we've all fought so hard to achieve. When everyone else was ready to admit defeat, you and WarDog persisted and won. I couldn't be prouder of you both."

My chest expands in pride as WarDog and I bask in our mate's praise.

"All that's behind us now. We can both just look ahead. You said you'd be my mate. Do you still mean it?"

"Yes." She snuggles closer and kisses me. It's a chaste kiss, but it promises so much more.

Willa

Even though Bayne was at death's door yesterday, miraculously he's fine now. He tells me it's his shifter nature that allows him to heal quickly. Wow, it would be amazing to be able to do that.

He pulls me onto his lap as we wait for the meeting to begin. I have no complaints. Besides, it's standing room only in here. Between the inhabitants of both ships, the women from the dorm, and seven of the eight males who had been locked in that horrible underground dungeon, we've got a full house. A couple of hours in the regen tank has done wonders for all the males but So'Lan. Even though most are still too weak to be up for more than a few hours, all of them wanted to be here.

"Thank you all for coming," Zar says, a clutch of handwritten notes in his hand. "A few announcements first, some recreation I think you all will enjoy, then we have serious business to discuss. First I want to thank all the males of both ships who risked their lives on the mission yesterday. What a great success that all of Khour's males at the compound were eliminated and we were able to rescue the males and females who are with us today.

"The evil Daneur Khour, the male responsible for the capture, pain, and torture of almost everyone here and thousands more across the universe, died a death he deserved."

The noise of cheers, clapping, and stomping feet erupts in the room. Every male in the room stands, faces Bayne, nods, and thumps his chest with his fist in the gladiator show of respect. Bayne's humble nod of acceptance has my eyes filling with tears of pride.

When everyone settles down, Zar continues, "Many of you have asked about Wrage who was injured in the attack on Fairea. In case anyone failed to notice, he's recovering well and is with us today."

He nods toward the Wryth'N male who looks to be in great health when he stands and, just to show how strong he is, lifts his mate Elyse, who squeals in surprise. Although the group bursts with laughter, by the look on Elyse's face, he's going to get reamed out for that little stunt when they return to the cabin they share.

"And good wishes to Bayne, our very own WarDog, who escaped death and has also recovered."

The males stomp their feet, the women clap and cheer, and Bayne looks at the floor. Is he embarrassed? He looks so cute; I think he's blushing under all that gorgeous tan skin.

"Regarding So'Lan, the Ton'Arran we rescued from the dungeon, Dr. Drayke says the male is still in . . ." Zar shuffles through his notes, "critical condition. For those of you who have a relationship with your Gods, I'm sure the male would welcome your prayers."

The room grows silent for a moment. Every one of us has heard of the deplorable conditions in which he and all those males were held. It's brutally obvious looking at the emaciated, injured, and sickly males scattered throughout the room. The women we rescued look to be in better physical condition but their hollow eyes suggest there's more to the story.

I can hardly fathom what they all have been through. I know many in this room can relate to the abuse they've endured. I imagine I'm not the only one thinking, 'there but for the grace of God go I'. We're all so lucky to be free. And now free of the MarZan cartel that has been pursuing us and preventing us from feeling the true peace of freedom.

"I thought we'd all enjoy a bit of entertainment. I believe there isn't a soul in the room who wasn't abused or terrorized by Daneur Khour and the MarZan cartel. We pulled the vid feed from the mansion.

"Anya told me to warn you . . ." After consulting his notes, he says, "This is R-rated and those of you with . . ." he shuffles again, "weak stomachs may want to close your eyes or step out of the room. That's because we're going to watch what Bayne and WarDog did in that mansion on Fairea. It was all recorded."

He peers over his sheaf of papers at the audience. None of us get up to leave.

"Willa, you won't like this," Bayne says. "Please leave."

"Why? You won. I may see you injured, but I know the ending. You got your revenge."

"I . . ."

Did I think he was embarrassed a moment ago? He's positively distressed now.

"I was bloodthirsty. You won't love me after you see this. Please step out." His lids slam shut as if he's remembering something he'd rather forget.

Frankly, I'd love to see the bastard get what he deserved. Not only was he directly or indirectly responsible for enslaving me and everyone on board, but what he did to those males they carried up from under the ground? That alone should earn him the very-excruciating-death-penalty. But Bayne doesn't want me to watch, so I won't. I don't want to cause him any more pain. I give him a swift kiss on the lips and say, "Nothing you could do to that bastard would be bloodthirsty enough, in my opinion, but I'll step out."

I make my way through the double doors and wait until the vid is over and the appreciative catcalls, wild applause, and stomping die out, then return to sit back on his lap.

"You have a good male," one of the women calls to me as I make my way through the audience to Bayne. Several women vehemently agree.

I glance at Shadow. Word has it that Khour was indirectly responsible for the loss of his eye and arm as well as for his parents selling him into slavery. His nostrils are flared and he's breathing heavily. Petra's holding his hand as if her life depends on it, but in actuality, *she* is *his* lifeline.

"I'd like a copy of the vid," he murmurs to Zar. "I'd like to watch it one or two hundred more times."

Now that I'm seated, all I can see is his back. His shoulders are still heaving as he breathes heavily. "I hope this gives him the closure he needs," I whisper to Bayne.

Zar must have amazing hearing, because he says, "Sextus also mentioned getting closure when we sent a copy of the vid to our pirate friends."

The two captains now get to the heart of the matter. We have to decide what to do with the new souls aboard our ships. There are a thousand details involved in the logistics of absorbing so many new people.

After an hour of discussion, a plan begins to form. None of the new males or females are particularly keen on roaming the galaxy on either of our vessels. I think we're all in agreement on that because most of us were wondering how we could assimilate so many people at once—none of whom appear to have any skills that would be helpful to us. Besides, none of the males have fully recuperated yet.

Only one male thinks he might be welcomed back onto his home planet. He'll contact them soon and one of the ships will reunite him with his kin if that's the plan. The others were either sold into slavery by their families or will be outcasts when they return after such long incarcerations. Of course, we all know none of the Earth women can return home.

There's a perfectly good compound on Fairea. Shadow is confident he could forge a bill of sale giving us rightful ownership. It has a fully-equipped medical facility, a *ludus*, space vessels, gardens, and plenty of housing. These people could be self-sufficient in the compound if they want, but they're also close to hospitals, markets, and merchants.

One of the males informed us he's a trained medic and will be able to continue the care Dr. Drayke started for all the males and females who will settle there. There are many settlements on Fairea, including the one that has the Renaissance-like fair. So everyone has the freedom to stay in the compound or relocate somewhere else.

Most of the newcomers are so traumatized they can't think much farther than having a safe place to sleep every night, but a few mentioned they might have skills that will come in handy on the planet. Dawn, a perky girl with the slightest southern accent asked if she could raise chickens. If circumstances were different, we could probably be friends.

There's a great deal of discussion, especially about the fact that they all experienced abuse of some sort down there.

"The land didn't harm us, nor did the buildings," Thran says. He seems to be in the best shape of all the rescued gladiators. He's of the same race as Ar'Tok with his curved horns and dreads that move, except his skin is burnished bronze and his horns are almost golden. He's a proud, handsome male. "And the people who did harm us are dead." He's not a big talker, but he seems particularly happy to have said that last sentence.

"We can put all that behind us," says Naomi as she primly sits in her chair, acting as if it's a throne. She's the oldest on board, looking to be in her 40s. "There are numerous ways for us to earn money there, and the compound is easily defensible, that's why Khour owned it."

One of the other new women, Melodie, mentioned Naomi had regular private meetings with Khour. Although she looks innocent, something tells me there's more to her than meets the eye.

Soon, all the newcomers are in agreement with the idea of claiming the compound on Fairea as their own. No one feels trapped or without choices, which was the deciding factor for everyone.

"All right," Zar says seriously as he reorganizes his papers, "let's put this to a vote."

Although I wouldn't have thought a room full of this many people could arrive at a unanimous decision, that's exactly what happens.

"We've been through a lot," Dusty, one of the new women says, her voice pregnant with unspoken meaning, "I've been researching Fairea since I've boarded the ship. Humans aren't illegal there. Perhaps once we get our shit together we could be a beacon of hope for not just humans, but any who escape their cruel masters. I'd like to call our new home Sanctuary."

A little thrill zings through me as I imagine what it would feel like if I hadn't been rescued. If I had been a slave on some planet with an awful master and one day someone whispered the word 'sanctuary' to me. It would be like a secret hope I could nurture in my heart. It would have given me the will to survive, the desire to live.

"I love the name," I say loudly. It's my first comment of the day, but I repeat it, "I love it."

While everyone is agreeing, Beast interrupts to say, "We've got our work cut out for us. We want the newcomers to have the best start possible. We're not leaving this sector until the compound is clean and functional."

"If I'd known this was going to happen," Stryker announces loudly, "I wouldn't have painted every wall in every room with my enemy's arterial spray."

Gross as that is, I find it hilarious. So does everyone else.

~.~

"How come we're the lucky ones assigned to this room?" I ask as I look around Daneur Khour's bedroom—or what's left of it.

"You saw yourself that they pulled names out of a kitchen pot."

"I still wonder if they rigged it somehow," I grouse.

"Consider yourself lucky that a few of the gladiators volunteered to remove all the bodies first."

"Right. Glass half full."

He cocks his head with a quizzical look.

"There's always something to be thankful for," I amend.

Although there are no dead bodies in this room, there's a lot of blood. From where the wooden wall was sprayed with laser fire, there are enough shards to build a life-sized model of the empire state building.

"All work and no play makes Jack a dull boy," I say, even though I know Bayne won't understand a word of it. This is our fourth day on Fairea and all we've done is clean up the mess from the attack. My arms ache and I'm sick of the sight—and smell—of blood.

"We're making progress," Bayne says without complaint.

"I know, but when we hovered past the Fair area I thought it would be fun to attend. All we've been doing is working."

He says nothing, just keeps shoveling wood chips into trash bags, but I suddenly listen to the words coming out of my mouth. I'm complaining about a little cleanup work when the males I care about almost lost their lives here? I clamp my whiney little lips together and redouble my efforts.

"I like everyone on the *Fool's Errand*," Bayne says abruptly. He's not a big talker, so I have a feeling something important is coming. "Same with the *Devil's Playground*."

"Me, too."

"But I'm thinking we have an opportunity we should consider. All the new people will be staying on Fairea, and I'm wondering if we should stay, too."

I shove the last of Daneur Khour's clothes into a trash bag and turn to look at Bayne.

"I think I would like it here. We could make a home for ourselves. WarDog could run and play. I could hunt. We could create . . . a family here. It wouldn't work as well on a ship; that would be hard for canines." His gaze pierces mine. He's serious.

"You've given this a lot of thought," I hedge. Then I wonder why this hasn't already occurred to me. I'm a farm girl—born and bred. I like to tend herds of animals and gardens. There was nothing—not one job—that was a fit for me on the *Fool*.

And WarDog. Of course, the big lug would do better gamboling in a forest than traipsing the metal corridors of a ship.

Bayne must think I hate the idea, because he presses on. "We don't know any of these people, but we will. We didn't know anyone on the *Fool's Errand* or the *Devil's Playground* a few *lunars* ago either. This will give us both a fresh start." He looks at me, his golden eyes alight with passion.

My mind bounces back to one word he used—family.

"Create a family, Bayne? We've never talked about it."

His jaw slackens and his face falls. "You don't want babes?" he asks, incredulous and sad. His gaze flicks back and forth across my face as if he's trying to discover if perhaps he read me wrong.

"Yes, I want babes. I want happy babes and mischievous toddlers and sullen teens. I want it all. And I want pets, and herds of animals that would be right at home in all those barns and fields, and corrals out there.

"And I want you, Bayne." I add softly, "You promised me a mating ceremony." I want to press my palm to his beautiful cheek, but don't want to sully him with a hand that just touched something belonging to Daneur Khour.

"Yes, Love. It just seemed you were so tired every night from cleaning up the compound."

I pout, wondering if he'll laugh at my hurt feelings, but he takes me seriously. "Tonight," he promises. "No matter how tired we might be, we'll mate tonight."

He steps over a pile of pillows, gently lifts my chin with one finger, and leans to kiss me.

"Yes, Love, tonight." Happiness bolts through me.

~.~

"So this big mating ceremony we've been putting off, it involves no other people?"

"No."

"No officiant?"

"No."

"But we'll be taking off our clothes?" I lift one eyebrow and notice funny feelings swirling in my tummy, and below. We're kind of joking, but it also feels like foreplay.

"No clothes will be worn during this ceremony," he nods seriously.

"In your culture it's the sex that binds you? But we've already had sex."

He takes a deep breath. No, I'd call it heaving a sigh.

"You're not inspiring confidence, Bayne."

"On Skylose, mates in my tribe have sex, and during sex the male bites the female. It's at that moment the two develop a mindlink they share for eternity. The few males of my tribe who mated with Skylosian non-shifters turned their mates into shifters this way."

He pauses a moment for that thought to sink in. He's still waiting for my response, but nothing is sinking in. Mindlink? Is that a psychic connection? Okay, that might be cool. Didn't I envy Dr. Drayke and Nova? I saw them working on Bayne and thought it was amazing how they communicated wordlessly like a well-oiled machine.

But shifting? I'd be a . . . dog? A very big dog? I remember the pain he was in after he shifted on Aeon II.

"Will it hurt?"

"To be honest, I don't know if you'll shift. You're not from Skylose. I don't even know if we'll develop the mindlink."

I look at my sweet mate as we sit at the little corner table in the cabin we share. Could I love him any more than I already do? I can't imagine it. Would I change even one thing about him if I could? Absolutely not. If he came to me as a mate without his inner canine, would that be better? No! Instead of making our relationship richer, it would be poorer, by far.

I love all of our differences—his pointed ears, those canine teeth, his pelt of fur. If this is the way of his people, then it will be my way, too. I secretly hope the shift doesn't hurt, but if it does, I'll embrace that too. The sacrifices I'm willing to make for him will be my way of declaring my deep and abiding love for him.

"I already said yes to being your mate, Bayne. But now that you've given me full disclosure I give full consent. I'd be honored."

I never thought his eyes could look more golden, but they do. They shine brightly for me.

"Part of the mating is for you to tell this to WarDog," he says seriously.

I'm surprised. I've never been sure how much Bayne understands in his canine form—how sentient he is.

"I'm all-in," I tell him with a smile and a nod.

Bayne steps out of his chair, removes his clothes, crouches, then turns into my favorite hound. I recall the first shift I witnessed, when he morphed from canine to humanoid in the dark catacombs on Aeon II. It was painful and left him panting on the filthy floor.

This shift is easy, and a happy two-hundred-pound animal greets me with a huge canine smile. He wanders over, sits between my feet, and puts his front paws in my lap. His mouth is slightly open, and he's looking at me expectantly. As momma used to say, 'somebody's home and the lights are on'. There's a smart being inside that shaggy head.

"I love you, WarDog." I don't feel silly saying this. In fact, it feels right.

He licks the back of my hand where I'm holding his paw, then nuzzles me with the depth of affection he's shown me since the first moment we met on that abominable slaver ship. I might not have received all the love he gave me from the start, but I realize he's always bombarded me with it.

"I'm going to be so happy to be your mate, too."

He chuffs, then as quickly as he appeared, Bayne reappears.

I'm not even sure how I wind up on his lap. But I'm here in the heavenly warmth of his embrace. His cock kicks hard at my hip, and his mouth devours me, his tongue excavating the warm depths of my mouth.

We've been honeymooners for days—or as he would say, sweetmooners—exploring each other, learning each other's secret places, how to prolong our ecstasy, and the words that elevate the mundane to the incendiary.

Somehow I think we're about to take our physical relationship to a whole new level, although I wonder how that's even possible.

I straddle him in the small chair, not caring for either of our comfort, needing only some means of getting closer.

His jutting cock presses the seam of my sex as I ride him, my fingers biting into the pelt on his shoulders.

Sex is different with Bayne. I love the delight he bestows, but he's the first sex partner I've had where his pleasure is infinitely more important to me than my own.

"Tell me what you want, Love," I demand as I arch my back, thrusting my breasts in his face. He has to be able to see my hardened nipples through my bra and t-shirt. "Want it hard? Soft? Fast? Slow? Quiet? Or do you want words?"

He gives me that lambent look that hints WarDog is as close to the surface as his inner being can get. I'm mating them both. I understand it now. I embrace it.

Instead of a verbal answer, he shows me as his calloused palm caresses my nape, his head bends to my level, and he kisses me as long and sweet and slow as two people can kiss.

Slow and silent—I get it. That's what he wants, that's what he shall have. My tongue greets his with lingering, heartfelt strokes. What's going on above the waist is achingly sweet and intimate. What's going on below the waist, however, is carnal as I feel every pull and drag of his hardened cock on my clit.

One minute more of this, two at the most, and I'll be announcing my first orgasm of the evening with a moan— and I'm still fully clothed.

He knows the minutiae of my response cycle better than lovers I've had for years. Maybe he's more attentive than anyone I've ever shared a bed with, or maybe it's that canine nose. It doesn't matter, I want him more right this minute than I've ever wanted anything in my life.

He scoops me into his muscular arms and carries me to the bed, but sets me on the floor when we're inches away. He pulls off my plain black t-shirt and bra with the utmost care, as if it's part of a religious rite. Perhaps it is.

Hooking his thumbs in the waistband of my pants and panties, he sweeps them down and pulls them off me, letting them lie on the floor near my top.

He takes my hand and leads us to the bed, making certain that we're both even, not wanting to take the lead tonight. We're coming together consciously. Both of us are making the choice to mate for life. It doesn't scare me like the idea of 'until death do you part' did on Earth. I welcome it.

I lie on the bed and he straddles my waist. While kissing and nibbling my throat, he arouses the hardened nubs of my breasts until I'm incapable of thought. Then he places himself at my entrance. I'm so slick, so ready, he could slide in to the hilt in one swift move.

But it isn't like that tonight. He thrusts so slowly I can feel each of his bulges as they breach my entrance.

"That's right, Bayne. Welcome home." I glance at him and catch the smile that flickers on his lips. This male loves me, and my acceptance of him and everything he is is magic. For both of us.

He develops a rhythm so slow it's maddening, but like everything else tonight, I embrace it.

I feel the tingle of impending orgasm whirling in my belly. He feels it too, or maybe it's his sixth sense. Instead of forging ahead, though, he slows, then stops and drops a kiss on my lips.

"This way," he says as he pulls out long enough to flip me over onto my stomach, then lifts me by my hip bones.

Of course, I should have known this would be doggy style. How fitting.

He slides back into me in one quick thrust as if we were never apart. The moment changes. Instead of feeling like we should be in a cathedral, we're solidly in lust territory now. The long, slow thrusts are a memory as he slams into me. Only one hand holds me up from under my stomach, he's using the other to circle my clit.

My orgasm is building, and I can tell it's going to be a lightning storm of need and pleasure. Then his jaw clamps onto my shoulder. At first, his teeth are covered by his warm lips, but when I begin rocking back against him, trying to bury him into the depths of me, he exposes them and the sharp tips of his fangs make themselves known.

It pricks. I wouldn't even call it pain. I'm not sure this is the bite he warned me about, or if there's more to come.

My orgasm is swirling and building, ready to explode, and I hear my own grunts as I press back against him as hard as I can, trying to push myself over the edge.

When the first spasm starts, his teeth press more deeply into my flesh. He warned me, and he was right. It hurts. The pain is so sharp my orgasm decides to retreat for a second. Then an explosion of bliss blasts through me.

It's so powerful that if one of his arms wasn't still holding me up I would collapse on the bed. White lightning flashes inside my head. I feel it in my brain, which detonates pleasure bombs exploding in chain reactions from the top of my head to the soles of my feet.

I was so busy rocketing to the clouds that I missed his ejaculation, but I realize now that he came a moment ago. I feel his warmth inside me—liquid proof that what just happened was real.

It's his saliva, or maybe his come or maybe the combination that set off an atomic bomb of bliss inside me. It doesn't matter. It's rapture. It's heaven. It's more pleasure than the human mind could imagine. He releases his teeth from my shoulder and licks the spot with soothing strokes even though the pain has long since vanished.

That good, Love?

"Wh-What?"

Just feel, my beautiful Willa. Just feel.

My internal muscles are still spasming as I'm dancing in the clouds when I realize my mate just spoke to me inside my head.

I love you, Bayne. Give me just a moment to enjoy every second of this.

And he does, still pumping into me in little pulses, drawing out the aftershocks of my pleasure. We're tied. I love this part. The enforced strokes and cuddles and the biologically imposed intimacy.

Biology doesn't have to force me to love you and stroke you, mate. I would do that whether we were tied or not.

Although I'm still panting, I'm breathing slower, deeper, returning to the here and now.

Precious, he says.

Beloved is my response. *When do I turn into a canine? I was scared to death of it, but now I can't wait.*

When he doesn't respond, I glance over my shoulder to look at him.

With Skylosians you would have turned by now, Love.

A wave of sadness unexpectedly gusts over me. We're so connected—mentally and physically—that I can't differentiate whether this is his sorrow or my own.

I'm so blessed to have you as a mate, Willa. I'm not sad.

We have a lot to learn, Bayne. The first thing I'm learning is that it's going to be hard to lie to each other. You're sad, so am I. It's okay to admit it.

"Let's give it time, Love. You're not Skylosian."

The swelling of his penis reduces, and he pulls out so he can turn me in his arms. He kisses my forehead as if I'm the most precious thing in the universe.

We have this, he says, *this mental link. And we have each other.*

He's so right. A few months ago we were bound for a slave auction without a friend in the world and nothing in our future but misery. I've found a way to contribute doing something I love. I have two males who love me and whose only desire is to protect me. We have friends and love and more blessings than we can count.

I lean to kiss Bayne's nose. Before I knew there was a Bayne, this is how I kissed WarDog. I got over the fact that it wasn't hygienic the first day I met him. It's our special thing. "I love you too, WarDog."

Love.

Is that you, Wardog? Really? We can communicate?

Yes. You're mine, Willa. My forever mate. I've loved you since the first moment we met.

And I you, big guy. And I you.

Epilogue

Two months later . . .

Willa

"Now that we've killed over a hundred tarantu-scorps, this is a pretty peaceful planet," I tell Bayne as we tramp through the woods.

"Yes, Love."

Have I told you lately how happy I am? I ask, a close-lipped smile stretched across my face.

I believe you mentioned it before, during, and after we made love this morning.

Am I mistaken or is there a slightly smug look on his face?

We hear a noise to our right. I'm not sure I heard correctly, but one glance at Bayne's ears which are pricked in that direction tells me something's out there. I grab my laser pistol more tightly as he nocks an arrow, but we both stand down when we see a little squirrel-like animal scurry across the forest floor.

We go hunting first thing almost every morning. Well, first thing after we make love. I remember being envious of Dr. Drayke and his mate Nova for how well they worked together due to their psychic connection. I never thought how handy it would be in the sex department, but being able to silently tell your partner when you want it softer or harder or a little to the right ensures maximum bedroom pleasure.

I wink at Bayne and he squinches both eyes at me in response. I don't know how a guy can be huge and masculine yet be adorable at the same time. Somehow, he pulls it off.

Our hunting trips have become fun for me. As long as I'm armed with a laser and not a bow and arrow, I feel confident when we hunt the tarantu-scorps. Actually, I feel more than confident, I feel competent—and proud that I'm pulling my weight.

It feels great to know we're ridding our forest of the creatures. It was a lucky break that Fairea was getting bad intergalactic press about the deadly animals—it was affecting their tourism.

It turns out Zar was correct in surmising that the tarantu-scorps, well he used their correct name, but I couldn't possibly pronounce the word he used, were not native to this planet and have been causing havoc since Khour brought them here a year ago. They had no natural predators and their population was expanding at an alarming rate.

The selfish asshole had them brought in for his hunting pleasure, not giving a damn that it upset the ecosystem for miles around.

The bounty we collect for every kill has been a bonus for our little band of friends at Sanctuary. We even collected credits for the ones we killed at the campsite after Callista forwarded satellite pictures to the Fairean authorities.

Every single one of us has worked our asses off over the last eight weeks—those that can. So'Lan is still recuperating in the infirmary, but thankfully he's progressing every day. One day when Bayne was visiting him, he asked if So'Lan would like to meet WarDog.

When he explained that it was actually thanks to WarDog that Bayne had discovered him barely alive in that black cell and that it was his canine that had ended Khour, So'Lan readily agreed. Now he asks for Bayne to shift every time he's there. Turns out that my big scary four-legged warrior has the heart of an emotional assistance animal. Well, I knew that, and I'm thrilled he's now helping someone else find comfort and strength.

Before we moved down here, I spent countless hours talking to Star, who's in charge of the hydroponic gardens on both ships. We poured over the Intergalactic Database and found some hearty fruits, vegetables, and legumes that will grow well here on Fairea. The timing couldn't have been better because we arrived at the perfect season to plant our crops.

Not only am I having a blast cultivating crops that I hope will get us through next winter, but I'm also working on animal husbandry, too. My ultimate goal is to raise enough *arlacks* to sell at the local market. For now, we've bought enough to begin a herd as well as feed everyone in the compound. They're as big as cows, but not quite as docile, and their favorite grasses just happen to cover our sizable south pasture.

Their meat is delicious, and their hides are strong and supple. Dawn said she met a male in the market when she takes in the extra eggs to sell, who works with leather. Sounds promising.

With Bayne's support, I've decided to achieve my dream and work toward my veterinary degree. It's a big step, and the program doesn't start for several months, but I've already been accepted.

My dyslexia was always a handicap, but this program is taught mostly by vid on the Intergalactic Database. The tests aren't timed, and with the use of the translator function, I'll be able to keep up with all the other students. There's a college nearby where twice a year an instructor will provide hands-on training. Although it won't be easy, I know I can do it. The prospect is exciting.

The wild game Bayne brings in from his hunts supplements what we're using from the *arlacks*. We feel a sense of accomplishment that we're both an important part of our group. Although he prides himself on his hunting ability, he's been invaluable tending the *arlacks* as well. It turns out WarDog is an amazing herder. His size intimidates the big animals and with me being able to mind link and communicate exactly what I need him to do we can move the growing herd quickly and efficiently. WarDog loves being able to contribute, and I enjoy watching him run to his heart's content.

I'd initially worried about group dynamics, but natural leaders have stepped forward, and our community is progressing nicely, although not without squabbles and pitfalls. A few people seem to be pairing off, and there are a few who can barely stand to be in the same room as each other. I guess that's to be expected in a group as large and diverse as ours.

The secret offworld trips that Naomi arranges have definitely piqued my interest. They return with scads of money, but I'm told information about them is on a need-to-know basis. They've also informed me I'm not on the need-to-know list. Those in the inner circle reassure me we're safe, so I guess I can handle being in the dark, even though my curiosity threatens to kill me.

It was a great idea to stay on Fairea, Love. I tell Bayne. *As much as I liked our friends on the vessels, I never would have been this happy on the ship. Digging in the dirt, helping birth ugly* arlack *babies, and watching my mate get to run on all-fours.*

I'm happier to have a bow in my hand and my feet on the land, he admits.

And my paws, WarDog chimes in.

Since we've seen no arthropods and the forest is safe, Bayne will be shifting any minute. We have a routine. When he runs off on four legs, I stand with my back against a tree, my laser in my hand, and I watch him until his tail disappears as he lopes away.

The tiniest pang of sadness pierces me because I know what's coming soon. I quit trying to hide my envy weeks ago, because when your mate can read your mind, keeping secrets is nigh unto impossible.

Although at first I wasn't sure I wanted to be able to shift, now I long for it. We both gave up hoping about a month after our mating ceremony. We seldom mention it anymore, which probably isn't healthy, but talking about it makes us both sad.

Bayne even offered not to shift because he knows it makes me hunger for something I'll never have, but what kind of person would I be if I asked for such a thing?

So I try to take joy in watching WarDog's enthusiastic play, and his unmuted happiness when he returns from a hard run.

I won't be long, Love, Bayne says. Perhaps he sensed that my melancholy is sharper today than usual.

Take your time. I love to watch you having fun. At least that's true.

He removes his clothes and folds them neatly in a pile at my feet, then swiftly shifts. WarDog laps at my hand, turns, and runs toward the sunny hillock about half a mile away.

My heart clenches in a potent combination of adoration and yearning. I love my two guys so deeply. I thank God every day that I found this depth of love.

Why did Bayne ever tell me I might be able to shift? Perhaps if he hadn't dangled it in front of me I wouldn't want it so desperately. But, I scold myself, he didn't dangle it to tease me. He was making certain I had informed consent before we mated.

I love you, I call in my mind, knowing they're about to leave telepathic range. Good. I don't want them hearing even a whisper of my morose longings.

I imagine what it would be like to run free like WarDog. What it would feel like to have four paws to press into the soft soil, or to smell every scent in the forest, or to run so fast my hair would whip in the breeze.

Then I feel an odd sensation deep in my belly, or is it my chest? It's warm and tight and swirly. My brain fogs over and I feel weak in the knees. The disorientation lasts a moment, and I shake my head trying to dispatch my confusion.

Am I shifting?

Yes. I hear the voice clear as a bell in my head. It's both foreign and familiar at the same time.

You're my inner canine? I hold my breath, hardly daring to believe.

Joy surges through me as I release a breath which becomes a squeal of excitement. *How do I do this?*

Easy, she says, *just let me out.*

Easy? Really? I shrug my shoulders and as I drop them, I relax and picture a door opening in my mind.

Yes. We're connected. You have me now. We'll always be together.

The door opens and she steps through.

I have just enough time to yank my tunic over my head before the shift slams into me in earnest.

When Bayne first told me about it, I had worried it would hurt. It *should* hurt when you consider the cataclysmic changes and strain it puts on the body.

My bones are morphing in size and shape, my internal organs are rearranging, and . . . holy shit, my teeth are elongating! But I just watch the changes. They aren't painful!

When it's supposed to happen, it doesn't hurt, my canine lovingly informs me.

She's beautiful. Her fur is a warm caramel, and her tail and mane are a mix of caramel and the same color brown as my hair. Her luminous eyes are the same brown as mine. When I compliment her, her gaze dips to the ground. She's a bit bashful. How cute.

I'm on all fours now. My vision is sharper, but colors are muted. My body feels large and powerful and strong. Amazing. I did it. I shifted. My canine barks in enthusiastic agreement, tail wagging with the same exuberance I've seen countless times on WarDog.

She can't stand still for one more second. Her urge to run can't be denied. It takes a few slow steps as I try to get the hang of all fours.

Stop directing me, she huffs good-naturedly. *Just let go, I've got this.*

Right. I let go. Then she's loping, and in less than a minute she's running, taking huge strides and barely panting with the effort.

Holy shit! This is magnificent! I'll never shift back.

Yes, she agrees.

I realize that although she's canine, she's never had a body to run in before, either. I'll just let her run and run until her body falls into a furry heap, and when she regains her strength we'll run again.

The smells! She smells everything. Everything. Every varmint and critter from here to Sanctuary and back. I smell the decomposing leaves and . . . I even smell the sunshine. Smells that were gross to my human nose smell wonderful now. Well, if not wonderful, then they certainly smell exciting.

I smell WarDog. It's as if he left a trail of neon blue smoke for me to track. It's ridiculously obvious. Why did I never notice this before? She follows it easily and we see that WarDog does not like straight lines. He veers off, inspecting every nook and cranny of this forest. She follows his trail and discovers all the cool things he found along the way.

There he is. Standing on the hillock in the sun, his nose pointed in the air. I wouldn't have understood yesterday, but now it's obvious he's smelling the sun. It's pungent and reassuring at the same time.

All of a sudden, I'm not content to watch from afar. We both feel the urgent need to run to him. I don't just *want* to be with him, it's a desperate, urgent demand.

I realize that even though we share the same body in different forms, our thoughts and emotions are separate but shared. I had no idea just how this was for Bayne and WarDog. It's amazing and intimate and confusing and comforting to know I will never again be alone. I'm slowly differentiating what I'm feeling and what is coming from my new and very special friend. That pressing, frantic, insistent desire is all hers.

I know the instant he senses her, and I watch as he turns his gaze in our direction. I've seen this look on his face a thousand times, but it's so much more expressive when I'm looking through the eyes of my canine form. He loves us. But now it's tinged with something else—desire.

He wants her. And she wants him. In my canine form, I think she desires WarDog as much as I desire Bayne.

This is the way it should be, Bayne assures me with the same feeling of wonder and surprise and delight that I am feeling

He runs to us. She holds back the urge to run and waits for him. He's approaching so fast his fur is sleaked back by the breeze he's creating.

Mate. Mine, he says.

Mate. Mine, she replies, unable to drag her eyes from her mate.

He's running so fast he has to skid to a stop when he arrives in front of her.

He play-nips her mouth, and she play-nips right back until he runs back onto the sunny hillside, and she runs after him.

Your name? he asks, cocking his head.

Willa? she answers, not having a proper canine name.

Can I call you Beauty? It suits you.

Oh yes, she sighs with a huge canine smile.

It is a perfect name for her. It shouldn't surprise me that WarDog is as loving and demonstrative as Bayne

Let's let them have this time Bayne voices in my mind.

Yes, I agree. I pull back so Beauty can fully experience the wonder of her mate while Bayne and I share in their delight. Certainly, WarDog has done this for us so many times before. They circle and play and bark at each other. I always wondered what dog noises meant. Now I know.

Watching them and experiencing them vicariously, I've never felt so free in my life.

Then she smells his desire. He isn't shy about sniffing her arousal either. She wants him. This will cement everything our relationship has been hurtling toward since the first moment we met in the cell on that slave ship. The three of us are in a relationship and this binds it more than any words can say. No, what am I saying? It's the four of us now.

Love, mine, mate, WarDog says as he climbs onto her back, his forearms pulling her toward him, his sex at her ready opening. His huge mouth bites into her shoulder, holding her, marking her.

Beauty welcomes him inside her body and basks in the feeling of connection until their act is complete. In long swipes, he licks her face and the bite marks that will stay to match the ones I proudly bear on my shoulder.

Somehow, Bayne and I are naked on the soft, green grass, our limbs entwined.

You shifted, Love, he says with a sated smile.

I'd given up hope.

Me too. But here we are. Mated shifters.

Our kids will be, too? I ask.

Perhaps. Will it matter?

I pull him so tight I half expect to hear the sound of bones breaking. *No. That's just a detail. None of it matters. Nothing. So long as we're together and we love each other.*

You're right. We have everything we need and everything we want, he says, his eyes luminous with love. *Let's go back to Sanctuary, we've got a herd to tend to. Do you have clothes?* He asks as he eyes me up and down.

A tunic. I imagine my pants are shredded.

We'll hide some clothes in the forest in case your next shift takes you by surprise.

I'm overcome by a bolt of love so strong it almost hurts as I realize this is my life. This is what I have to look forward to for the rest of my days. I have a purpose, a herd to tend to and gardens to weed. I have a home, a family unrelated by blood, the freedom to be who we really are, and a sanctuary in which to live.

And, I sigh, *I have a mate who loves me and always thinks of what he can do to make me happy as well as how to protect me.*

Yes, Love. He throws his arms around me and tugs me close.

We send each other mental images of our inner animals. Both are passed out in postcoital bliss with canine smiles on their faces. WarDog gets his happy ever after, too.

Six months ago I never would have dreamed of anything more than the life I had. Somehow, life conspired to gift me with so much more.

The End

Dear Reader,

I hope you enjoyed WarDog and Willa's journey. It was a lot of fun writing WarDog and Bayne's inner banter as well as the wonderful romance they enjoyed with their mates.

If you've been following our intrepid gladiators from the beginning, I hope Daneur Khour's death gave you a feeling of satisfaction. I tried to use restraint, so you didn't have to run for your barf bag, while still allowing you to feel the gladiators' triumph of defeating their mortal enemy.

Have you already figured out what's next in store? Stryker and Maddie's story is next (keep scrolling for their first chapter).

I also hinted at the new series in the Alanaverse—Sanctuary. I want Sanctuary to provide our gladiators with a home base, as well as a place for abducted females to dream about during their difficult captivities. What nefarious plans does Naomi have? What is to come of the poor debilitated Ton'Arr, So'Lan? Will our downtrodden folks ever catch a break and get a chance to have some fun at the Fairean fair? All good questions that will be answered in due time.

Instead of me begging, picture 200-pound WarDog with his cute golden eyes and his paws up in the classic doggy-begging pose. If he could talk, he'd be asking you to take two minutes out of your busy schedule to review his book on Amazon. Reviews are the kindest thing you can do for an indie author like me. It gives my work legitimacy and helps people new to my work feel confident to try me out. Thanks in advance.

Want to be the first to know about upcoming books, giveaways, cover reveals, and more? Subscribe to my newsletter. I won't spam you. For my latest contest, the winner got the name of her choosing as a character in an upcoming book! Fun, huh? You'll also get a copy of my free book, Terminus, which is Shadow's backstory. Subscribe here.

Sneak Peek of <u>Stryker</u> Book Thirteen in the Galaxy Gladiators Alien Abduction Romance Series

Chapter One

Stryker

Look at her. Gods, she's beautiful. Sometimes, when she lets me sleep in her cabin, I force myself to stay awake after sex. When she's fast asleep, I turn on the light in the refresher so it casts a glow into the room and I just watch her.

I love to look at her. She won't let me tell her she's beautiful. It's one of the many rules she laid down early in the relationship. I don't even know if I can call what we have a relationship. I'm not sure what this is. Other than that I love her.

I keep the lights off during sex. Another of her rules. I know she can't stand to see my face. Who would? It's badly scarred from injuries when I fought as a gladiator. They threw me in with that feline beast from Abachae without even a six-inch dirk to protect myself much less a sword to attack him with. I was badly mauled. I wouldn't look at my face either if I didn't have to. I understand.

My cock is hard already, even though we had sex less than an *hoara* ago. Shit. That's another of her rules. I called it making love once and that made her very unhappy. She didn't have to tell me not to say it again. The way the corners of her mouth turned down and her pretty brown eyes filled with tears was enough to make an impact even on my thick skull.

We've known each other for over an *annum*. I was on a space vessel on my way to a slave auction with nine other gladiators when our captors threw an Earth female into each of our cells. Within an *hoara* they forced us to mate upon threat of death.

She was terrified. I could smell her fear. Her eyes were so wide the white showed all the way around. I tried to put my head in the shadows so she wouldn't have to look at me. But that day I don't think she could have identified my face if pressed to do so. She was too busy looking at my cock. It scared her more than my face.

I waited as long as I could before I approached her, but we weren't given time to get to know each other. I was gentle and didn't hurt her. I talked to her and tried to calm her. It didn't work—she was petrified.

Later, she divulged how much she appreciated how hard I tried to calm her fears. Despite my efforts, she cried all through it, though, which made it difficult for me to stay hard. I've never found it arousing to hurt anyone. But we got through it and began an easy truce.

The gladiators staged a revolt within a week. We commandeered the ship and now we're speeding through the galaxy making money from gladiator matches where we get to keep our own purses. Almost all the money I earn goes back to the ship. My contribution makes me feel like I'm a part of something bigger than myself.

We've formed a family on this ship, as well as adding another vessel to our little armada. We're all escaped slaves just trying to stay one step ahead of the Feds and our former owners, the MarZan cartel.

Many of those original couples have formed permanent matings. Maddie and I, though, are what she calls 'fuck buddies'. I never let her know how this designation squeezes my heart. I just try to be the same Stryker I've always been. I'm a male who has a strong sense of right and wrong, and I'm loyal. It's my fondest hope that one day she'll want us to be more than fuck buddies.

I've bonded with her. I love her, although I know better than to say it. That's why I like to stay awake until she's sleeping heavily. I wind a strand of her springy brown hair around one of my huge fingertips, and I whisper how much I love her without fearing her rejection.

It doesn't matter how good I think we are together. She needs to feel that way, too. Obviously, she doesn't.

Although I don't understand why she rejects me yet shares her body with me, I sometimes get the feeling something eats at her from the inside. If she would only share her worries and concerns with me, I would be able to make everything better. I'm strong and fearless. If she would reveal what weighs on her so heavily, I will go to the ends of the galaxy to fix it.

I've asked, but she denies anything is wrong.

There's one way we're compatible. In bed. She seldom grants me permission to sleep with her, but she's never said no to sex. I love to provide her endless pleasure, and she's never failed to make me feel good. It's the one place she's giving. Generous in fact.

I press my nose under her ear and nuzzle her, then suck in a deep, humid breath. We've been together long enough that I know every move, every technique to arouse her. She loves to be awakened like this—fully ready for sex.

Once she even let it slip *why* she liked it. She said this way's the best because she doesn't get in her own way. I'm not certain what that means, but I think sometimes it's hard for her mind to shut down enough for the pleasure to take over. When she wakes up wet and wanting, though, she can dive into the act. Even though it's with me.

Maddie

I'm on fire. Oh, Stryker's doing it again. I love when he wakes me like this, my core already dripping wet, my nipples hard as diamonds, my hips thrusting. Sometimes I wake with a little moan on my lips, like now.

"Stryker," I whisper. He likes when I say his name. It's the least I can do to please him.

His thick, calloused fingers pluck my nipples just the way that quickens my pulse and makes me wet. I roll onto my back and open my thighs, giving him complete access to me.

"Maddie," he growls, biting back the things I know he wants to say.

Damn. It's going to be one of those nights. Sometimes I can shut out my shitty thoughts and just dive into the physical pleasure. I can already tell tonight won't be that night. The snakes in my head are coming out to play in full force. Screaming at me, chastising me, deriding me.

You're such a fucking bitch to him, one of my many inner critics scolds. Great. Even the heckler is on duty tonight.

I redouble my efforts to take pleasure from Stryker's sexy hands, his deep breathing, his hard cock pulsing against my thigh. When that doesn't stop the contemptuous voices in my head, I wiggle out of his grip and push him onto his back, then dive for his cock.

His hard cock in my mouth is one of the only things guaranteed to keep the crazy thoughts out of my head. Ahh, yes. It's working.

I love everything about this male's body. Every plane, every muscle, the shallow divots on his flanks, and the little ones on either side of the base of his spine. My fingers adoringly explore his ropey shoulder muscles. When we're not in the thick of things, I even like the soft hair under his arms. I like everything about this body.

It's hard and masculine and tastes good. Even when he comes in from the *ludus* after sparring. When he tries to jump in the shower before I attack him, I'll catch him just to snatch a taste of his salty tang.

I like his face. I know he's self-conscious about his scars, but I don't see them anymore. I just see the compassionate male beneath his skin. I wish I could see him now, but I can't bear to have the lights on during sex. I don't like the way I look, which makes it hard for me to find my pleasure. Since the lights are on now, I'll keep my eyes closed.

Right now, though, with his thick cock in my mouth, all the writhing snakes in my head are finally silenced. It's just me and him. A fucking miracle.

I cup his balls in my palm and roll them just the way he likes.

"Maddie," he says on a deep sexy groan.

That's right Stryker, no one deserves pleasure more than you. I swirl my tongue and roll his balls and then flick his frenulum; it's his very favorite place.

"You're trying to kill me, L—" He thinks he caught himself in time, but he just awakened all the snakes. Shit. I thought we were going to get to the finish alone this time-- just him and me without the snakes. Not tonight, I guess.

But he'll never know. I want him to think I didn't hear him almost call me 'Love'. In fact, I speed up, bobbing my head, moaning in pleasure, providing more pressure with my lip-covered teeth. He's panting, his thick fingers taking extra effort to be gentle on my shoulders, so I don't feel like he's forcing me onto his cock.

He doesn't need to compel me to do this. I love it. I love giving him physical pleasure. It's the only thing I'm capable of giving.

"Gotta slow down, Mads," he says as he flips me onto my back and maneuvers between my legs in one swift move.

Two hundred pounds of gladiator muscle is crouched between my thighs with one mission and one mission only. This man wants to hear me come.

He won't be satisfied with a faint little moan, either. He won't stop until I'm screaming loud enough for everyone on the ship to hear. We're a little family. My screaming orgasms quit embarrassing me before we even staged our insurrection, when we were in the cell block. There's no way to hide them, and they make him so fucking happy.

I guess a few good things came from his gladiator training. He has the stamina of five males, and he had to train with his non-dominant hand, so this male is ambidextrous in all the right ways.

He can finger fuck me with one, and practically bring me to orgasm with the other just plucking my nipples.

"You just keep getting better at that," I tell him between gasping pants as my head thrashes against the pillow. I pull my knees up, my heels flat on the mattress, and can't contain my urge to press his beautiful head even harder against my clit.

I come with a grunt, then a long, howling moan. Somehow, he knows what every wordless noise and changing pitch means. He knows when to get right down to business, and when to back off to prolong my ecstasy.

Tonight, I just want it hard and fast, and the red male is delivering it as if he had a written playbook.

He strings three orgasms together, first using one finger, then two, then a third. He does the come-hither thing just when I think I'm rolling to a stop, and amps me up for several more releases. It's only now that he gives me what I truly desire—that beautiful cock.

I'm slippery with my own release, he needs no help to enter me in one long, hard, delicious drive.

"That's right, Stryker. Right where you belong," I whisper as I feel my inner muscles quiver against him, setting off a chain reaction of explosions—mine and his. I love to feel his come jet into me. It never fails to make me feel so feminine, and somehow cared for and owned. The snakes always go away, at least for a moment, after he comes.

I pull him down onto me, our bodies hot and sweaty. I lick his pec with the tip of my tongue so I can go to sleep with his taste in my mouth.

I let him cuddle me after sex. It's the only time I allow it. And now the snakes come back to play, hissing at me, deriding me for 'allowing' anything in a relationship like this. I'm an awful person. I know it.

With two people, one shouldn't have power over the other. But it's the only way I can bear to be in a cabin alone with him. If he didn't follow my rules, my edicts, I'd never be able to tolerate him walking through the doorway.

~.~

I wake early, today like every day. Stryker's gone, just as I expected. I laid down the ground rules the day we were freed: no words of endearment, no praises about my looks, no sleeping over unless expressly requested, and if so, be gone when I arise.

Bitch, my heckler hisses.

No shit, is my honest reply.

I need to get going, an entire ship full of people are going to be in the dining room wanting breakfast in an hour and I don't have time to dawdle.

Except I can't force myself out of bed.

I knew this was coming. It's why I tried to keep him at arm's length since the day we met. I knew I could fall for him quick and hard if I allowed it. How could I resist the gentle giant? Look at his big, strong hands, yet they touch me with such exquisite tenderness. And the way he looks at me, the way he's looked at me almost from the moment we met. God, what woman doesn't dream of a male gazing at her with adoration?

I didn't want to taint him. I didn't want my snakes to infect him, too. But here we are. Does he think he's sly? Does he really think I don't know he sneaks into the bathroom at night and turns on the light just so he can look at me? Does he think his little slips where he almost says the "L" word trick me?

I know how he gazes at me with longing when he doesn't think I notice. And it breaks my heart that I can't reciprocate.

Hot tears flow down my cheeks. Tears of sadness. And self-loathing, too. Don't forget that.

I'm getting worse. I knew this was coming.

I've fought depression since my teens. It waxes and wanes. Some days are worse, some are better, but on the whole, the really dark times come every few years. Those are the periods when no meds help. There's no 'better living through chemistry' that I used to joke about with my friends.

No, there are periods that sometimes go on for years where I gut through the debilitating depression through sheer fucking strength of will. Today I can feel it coming after me fast and hard. And outer space doesn't have Prozac.

As much as I love the salty taste of Stryker's skin, I hate the salty taste of my tears. I pound my fist on my thigh and try to pull myself together.

I'm going to have to do it. I've avoided it since the first day we met. I thought if he followed my rules, we could keep what we have within my set parameters. But I've hurt him. I know it. I don't know how I deluded myself for a year, pretending what I was doing was okay.

Before I fall into the deep chasm of the worst of my depression, I've got to send him away. I've got to save him from me, protect him from the black hole of my emotions and my need. He's too good; he deserves so much better, better than me. I don't want to drag him down with me.

I hurtle off the bed, perform the world's quickest shower, and skid to a stop in my kitchen within ten minutes.

I cook breakfast, lunch, and dinner for all souls onboard every day of the year--nonstop. It keeps me as sane as I can get. And I get accolades, which helps, even if some days it feels like they're praising someone other than myself because I'm cocooned inside myself so far I feel hollow.

Around eight a.m. when everyone rolls in, I put on my Maddie persona and do my chef thing. As far as anyone on the ship knows, I'm the happiest female they've ever met. I don't talk, I sing. I think I developed it by watching Oprah who kind of sings her words sometimes. Only I do it constantly.

My depression is my little secret. No one knows. I didn't even divulge it to Dr. Drayke. I'm certain the galaxy doesn't understand human serotonin and dopamine. I mean, we're illegal up here, except that it seems everybody and their brother are abducting us.

"Biscuits and gravy," I call cheerily to the dining room, which is half full. "Eggs will be there in a minute."

Click on Stryker's cover to order now.

Galaxy Gladiators:

Zar and Anya—The feline captain of the *Fool's Errand* and Anya led the insurrection against their masters and freed all twenty slaves on the original ship. They are loving life mates.

Shadow and Petra—Shadow could pass for human except for his bionic parts, although he's from planet Morgana. His mate, Petra, is a hairdresser.

Tyree (Tie-REE) and Grace—Tyree morphed from a three-foot-tall non-sexual being to a huge alpha male. His mate, Grace is known throughout the galaxy for her ethereal musical compositions.

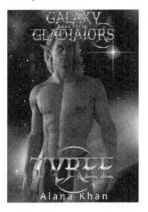

Devolose and Tawny—(Dev-AH-lose rhymes with dose) This mated pair left the Galaxy Gladiators to join Dev's cousin, Thantose, in the Galaxy Pirates series.

Dr. Drayke sun Omron (AHM-ron) and Nova—Nova came aboard after her arm was sliced off in a gladiator fight. Originally an MMA fighter, after she was abducted from Earth, she was trained as a gladiator. She now assists her mate, Drayke in medbay.

Axxios (AXX-ee-ose), Braxxus (BRAX-us), and Brianna—All males of this species are born as twins—one silver and one gold. The gold of the pair is more dominant. They fell hard for Brianna, a BBW massage therapist with a heart big enough to love them both.

Sirius (SEAR-ee-us) and Aliyah (aa·LEE·ya**)**—Born a geneslave with genetic material from different animal species, Sirius found his mate on planet Nativus. Aliyah was an Earth girl abducted young and nurtured by her native father. Her mother and father's story is told in the novelette, Jax-Xon.

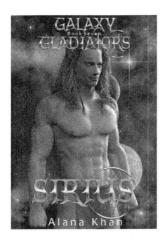

Dax and Dahlia—Dahlia was ripped from her life on Earth just days before her wedding. She had to adjust to life in space before she could realize how compelling her feelings were for huge gladiator, Dax.

Beast and Aerie (EH-ree)

Beast and Aerie joined the crew when they and three others were rescued from a slave ship. Beast is a Premier Gladiator (one of only ten in the Galaxy), and Aerie was stolen from her life as a Sports Attorney. She had a love for

Louboutins and now prefers flipflops with chartreuse alien eyes.

Ar'tok (ARE-tock) and Star

Ar'Tok had just been freed from jail right when he was rescued from a slave ship along with Beast and Aerie. A shy male, he meets human Star through midnight comms. Their love blossoms concurrent with Wrage and Elyse's book. This couple are not in the bang district, though. They're on the more respectable part of the planet. Happy Blessed Peace Day.

Wrage (Rage) and Elyse (uh LEASE)

Recently freed from slavery as a gladiator, Wrage heckles Elyse mercilessly in her position as a slave singing in a bar. Elyse agrees to Wrage's drunken marriage proposal, believing it will garner her freedom from both him and her owner. Little do they know that on the Pleasure planet there is no such thing as divorce.

Galaxy Pirates:

Sextus (SEX-tus) and Lexa

Sextus and Lexa begin on very bad terms and are throw together on a planet where she has to be subservient to him. He redeems his previous bad behavior by risking his life to save her. They were mated on his planet, Ceruleous.

Thantose (THAN-tose) The 'th' is pronounced like the 'th' in thought and Brin

The captain of the pirate ship had no desire for a mate until his protective instincts, and libido, were brought to life by Brin. Thantose is known for his love of theft, credits, the game of *klempto*, but most all his love for his mate.

Ssly (rhymes with fly) and Carrie

Ssly, a hover-chariot racer, keeps to himself to care for his adopted human daughter, Tru. He wants nothing to do with Carrie but needs her help to get Tru the medical help she needs. The two fell in love and the little family settled on Ssly's home planet.

Slag and KJ

Slag is the green, pebbled giant so debilitated by the effects of the irradiated green salt ore he can't talk and barely think. KJ is thrown into the mine as punishment by her new owner. Together they fall in love and go on adventures. One of which involves the adorable dreambaby pictured here.